Once
upon
a
Time
on
Grateful
Dead
Tour
Trina Calderón

Once Upon a Time on Grateful Dead Tour

ISBN 979-8-218-39744-9

Cover Art & Illustrations: Skye Cochran
Title Page Art: Harvest
Book Design: Miah Jeffra
Cover Design: Edgar Torres

Published 2024 by Trina Calderón

Deadicated to the kids, the ones on the dance floor,
the ones I lost touch with, the ones I always see again on the road,
the ones locked up,
the ones who left the building ...
to the trusty big sis co-pilot Liz (thanks for the tape),
to the tour dogs and cats,
to the Disco Bus, to the Pranksters, to the Hog Farmers, to the Wharf Rats,
to the swinger boys that were too hard to handle (you know who you are),
to the Rastas, to the bikers, to the poets,
to liberation and freedom,
and to all of us who continue to spread the light and love.
This darkness got to give!

Once Upon A Time on Grateful Dead Tour

Table of Contents

Foreword

Jerry Garcia once said, "Following the Grateful Dead is truly the great American adventure!" For those of us that tapped into the Grateful Dead zeitgeist, we completely understand what that means. Whether you saw the Dead only a few times, or hundreds, you most likely have a memorable story to tell. If you don't have a story, maybe you played it too safe? No risk, no reward. Once you found this scene and went deep down the rabbit hole with the songs they sang, it was pretty easy for us to start living out the stories of those songs! Hunter and Barlow wrote about outlaws and gamblers, lovers and thieves, and of course, mystical creatures, and all of those things rang true with us. We WERE drug dealers (outlaws), we all had lots of lovers, we probably gambled for real or metaphorically, and of course we lived by the rule of the unicorn who was really a "dragon with matches." My personal Grateful Dead adventure was grand! I wouldn't change a thing! We drove long distances to shows from Maine to Florida, San Diego to Alaska, and everywhere in between, all while channeling the spirit of Neal Cassady, sold drugs, got pulled over in Nebraska and Missouri with enough drugs to put us in jail forever, but somehow thru the sheer magic of Grateful Dead Energy we skated by...until we didn't. I went to prison for possession of LSD with intent to distribute, I was one of the lucky ones who got busted before the evil Reagans declared their "war on drugs" and locked people up for decades. I got out, and still was able to have a real life, and tap back into the Grateful Dead experience in a meaningful way without being an outlaw. I brought a camera along with me, so my stories also have the photos to help the third eye see the experience along with the words telling you about the experience. I was saved by photography, and now when we look at these photographs from 35 to 40+ years ago, we see US, whether we are in the photos or not. The stories on these pages—which are written as fiction but based on real events—are vivid tellings of the many adventures that we all had because of our love for the Grateful Dead. Whether you can find a little piece of yourself in these stories or not, just like the photographs, you are part of the swirly story that collectively proves this truly was the great American adventure. We all had parallel experiences against the backdrop of a group of musicians that changed the way we all view the world and with the help of the stories they sang to us in song we are now better, wiser, and more evolved human beings...Psychedelics and the Grateful Dead will do that to you. Enjoy reading these stories from the wandering mind of Trina, they shed light on a unique subculture, and you just might find a little bit of yourself in between the lines...Light the song with sense and color...

Jay Blakesberg
San Francisco, CA
March 2024

The Hug

"We're going to miss the BART back to the city," Gus complained to his brother Jason. Heather and Kelly squirmed around next to them, unsteady, with muffled excitement and hope. They arched their necks thinking the extension could give them a new view, a special vantage than what was entirely indifferent to anyone else at this particular moment. The show was over, everyone was glowing, and this small group was living for the next rush. It was all about to go down, because a fancy black stretch limo was sitting there too, waiting, just like they were.

"Soon, watch," Heather said.

"Well, hot damn, there you go!" Jason exclaimed. Sure enough, there he was. He walked right out of the back of the Greek Amphitheatre, and came right over to them, as if a tractor beam of love showed him the way. Katie smiled huge and he hugged her, then Heather, Gus, and Jason. Lovely, meaningful, connecting hugs.

"Take us with you!" Heather begged.

He chuckled, it's appreciated and sweet. "You know, I want to. I would, but every time I do that nowadays it ends up in the papers. Sorry." The limo driver opens the door and Jerry steps inside his plush ride. The limo pulls away safely into the starry Bay Area night.

Where's the Car?

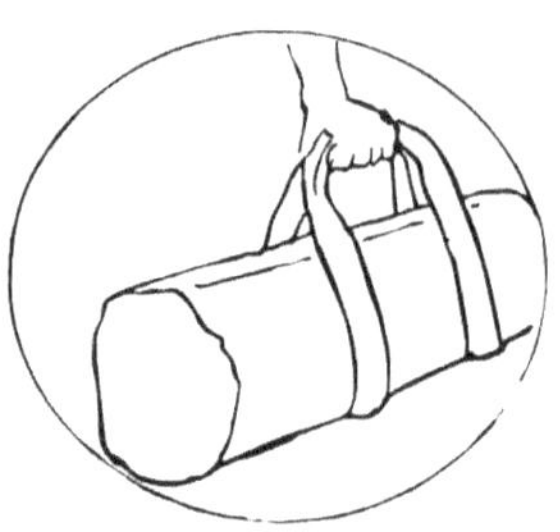

Mirabelle was quiet and cute. She had long blond hair, and sweet brown eyes. Not like other girls, but not from tour or the streets. Jared found her in Tennessee, the last time he was back home after the harvest season in Oregon. He wasn't a farmer, but he could get rid of weight quick and made the back and forth as much as he could.

Jared was an old friend of Frank's from tour, a little older, and Valerie could tell since the first time he came over that Frank looked up to him. She adored most of the boys, they were her brothers and they treated her with respect because she could hold her own on the street, was a good cook, and because she put up with Frank who liked to drink himself into a dark shadow some days. He had pissed their bed more than once, but she loved him from the day he rode up to her on the street on his mountain bike.

She was walking down 13th Street and he spotted her from a block away, enchanted by her long dark hair, high cheek bones, and mysterious dark brown eyes. It was love at first sight and he didn't care what her story was, he was writing himself into it. It was his Harley-Davidson belt buckle, faded Levi's, and shoulder-length light brown hair that got her attention. He looked like a young Bob Weir, circa '67, from a black and white photo she always loved. Spitting image kind of, with a funny childish aura. Frank's brown eyes hypnotized her. He wore a homemade green and brown corduroy hoodie, with long sleeves and pockets. A swinger boy born and raised in the redwoods; all she could do was swoon. On that delicious Indian summer afternoon, he walked her home, holding his bike alongside her 'til they got to the east side of town.

About eight months later, Frank and Valerie were living off 16th and High Street, far enough away but close enough to the action, and their favorite brewery. Frank could be a loose cannon, but he did business right, and helped a lot of the kids out. Valerie had the same kind of heart and together they were a ruckus on the bottle, but kind when it came to family. Brothers were always welcome on their way through town, if they needed to get some headspace or even hide out, Valerie was usually happy to have them.

Jared and Mirabelle were two peas in a pod. She was different but they were connected. Valerie wondered if he saved her from some awful situation in Tennessee, but she didn't ask, at least not yet. She made them some tea and some avocado hummus sandwiches with delicious fresh tomatoes from Saturday market. Frank told them stories to pass the time and always had a punchline for every ending. He knew how to make the room laugh; he lived through so many bizarre happenings; Valerie learned something new about him damn near every day when he went on talking. That kid survived icy bus crashes during winter tour, guns pulled on him on the Haight, crazy arguments with Hells Angels his truck driving mother used to date, and all kinds of stupid shit like scabies and head to toe poison oak. She loved him so much he got a tattoo of her eyes on his forearm.

Mikey and Kenton came by with some beers and the afternoon took a welcome turn. They were all waiting on Tristan who was on his way with herb. Everyone needed to reup and get back out soon. Even Valerie had some college custies blowing up her pager. Youngster Gus had stopped by earlier, waiting on work from Jared. Valerie wanted to let him in to wait but Jared told her they needed to lock it down.

Mirabelle was having fun, though she didn't drink. Mikey packed his glass, and she did partake in the smoke. Valerie could tell she was learning the ropes, and probably hadn't ever left Tennessee on her own. She wanted to know more about her but couldn't get a word in over Frank.

An hour or so later, Tristan knocked at the door.

"Yeah, here you are," Jared greeted him. "Come in here, brother." Calm and collected, Tristan had a duffel bag filled with weed. They circled up and the first thing he did was pull out his pipe.

"Let's puff, these nugs are so kind. Smell." He opened his nug jar and handed it to Valerie, like a gentleman. She smelled some divine grass, her mouth watered. They passed the pipe around and got lit. Everyone was happy, this herb was going to fly and be good headstash.

"I'm gonna get a backpack, be right back." Jared kissed Mirabelle on the cheek and went outside. Less than a minute later, he came back inside. "My car is gone."

"What?" Frank said. He came to the door, and they stood outside.

"It's gone. I parked it right there."

"What the fuck? Are you sure, man?"

"Yes."

Mirabelle got up and looked outside. "That's where it was. What do you think happened?"

Jared started to boil, his temper was sublime but as soon as it ignited, there was no question there was going to be trouble. One thing about these brothers, they could be kind and gentle, and whoop some ass if necessary. Mikey, Kenton, and Tristan got up on their feet. At about six feet tall, and a couple hundred pounds, Kenton wanted to muscle the problem, and he had his Chevy Van parked a block away. "What do you think?" he questioned.

"I don't know. No one knows that car, it's her car," Jared said. Mirabelle was steady and concerned, she absolutely looked to her man for their next move.

"Anyone looking for you?" Frank said.

"Nope. No reason. We snuck in town and came straight here."

"Well, let's go fucking get it," Kenton said. "This town ain't that big." The boys split and took off to find the car.

Valerie cleaned up the kitchen and lit a cigarette and gave one to Mirabelle. She wasn't even sure if she smoked, but she took it. "So, what part of Tennessee you from?" she asked her.

"Maryville, outside of Knoxville," she told her.

"Oh, okay. I've driven through there."

Mirabelle was quiet. She was incomplete without Jared.

"How'd you meet Jared?"

"At a bar I was working at. A small dive, we served burgers, fries, and milkshakes. He came in to eat."

"Was it love at first sight?" Valerie wondered.

"It was. He's not my type usually, but he was so sweet. My boss was kind of a dick to him, didn't like the way he looked, but he stayed anyway and drank a few beers and waited for me to get off. He took me for ice cream, and we talked and talked. He was staying at a motel nearby, so I spent the night with him."

"How romantic!"

"It was," she said. "In the morning we went out for breakfast, and he told me he'd give me everything I ever wanted."

"He did?" Valerie teased.

"Yep," she laughed. "I quit my job that afternoon and we left for Nashville. Then we drove all the way to Santa Fe, New Mexico and he showed me all around, it's so beautiful there. I never seen anywhere like that that, how its desert and then these spectacular mountains, and the river. And all the peach adobe houses."

"Wow, how cool. You kids went on your honeymoon already," Valerie joked.

"Yeah, it felt like that." She smiled wide and blushed remembering how Jared had taken a hold of her. Every night they couldn't get enough of each other, and she loved his outlaw life, it was the adventure she never knew she wanted.

"Aww, Jared is sweet. He's soft-spoken, I always like when he's in town because he keeps it quiet. Some of the boys like to get loud with Frank, like Mikey. Those two keep me up all night sometimes, they get so rowdy. I gotta kick 'em out to walk their shit off but then they always come back with more beer," she laughs and rolls her eyes.

"I hope they find the car. I don't know what we'll do without one."

"Yeah, it's been awhile, right?" Valerie looked at her pager. Forty minutes had passed. "Where else has he taken you?"

"We went to Las Vegas!" she says. "I'd never been, and he said it was dumb, but I wanted to go so he took me."

"Oh my god! That's hilarious," Valerie said. "Where'd you stay?"

"Caesar's Palace. We only stayed one night," she said.

"Jared's so classy, how fun."

"Yeah." She was short on words for much really, but Valerie liked her innocence and was genuinely happy she got out of some rinky dink bar for brighter days.

There was a knock on the door, and Valerie could hear Frank whistle. He always whistled for her on the street if they were separated. She hopped up, opened the door and the boys burst in. They were almost feral; a chill had set in, and she could feel it on Frank's skin when he took her close and kissed her. Mikey shut the door and they all sat down, ready to get back to exactly where they left off.

"You find the car?" Mirabelle asked Jared.

"Yes, baby." He handed her the keys and kissed her on the lips.

Valerie looked at Frank and as she started to ask, "What--," he shot her a look that said, 'don't worry about it and not another word.' She stared back at him and saw a smudge of dirt and blood on his neck. She brushed it off, kissed the spot and handed him a cigarette.

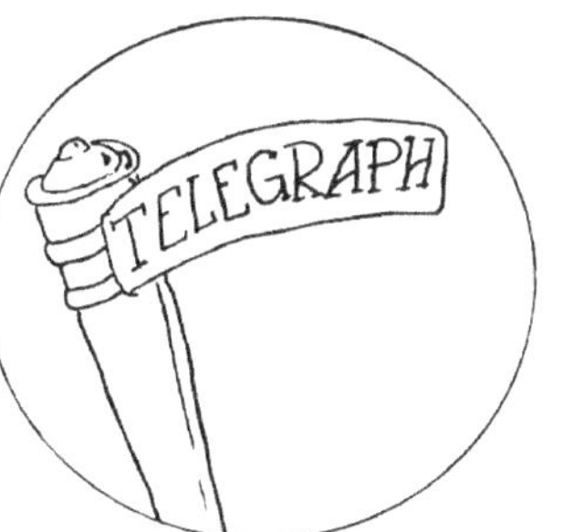

He Left His Body in Bezerkley

The late afternoon is carefree on Telegraph Avenue. Cars whiz by, students make their way to the university, civilians inhabit their blue-collar jobs, and the suits are in and out of fancy offices. The ancient sun stalwart, time directs this daily population. On the dirty street, telephone poles have flyers stapled up like wallpaper and graffiti crowds city utility boxes. The BART is not far, with stairwells infested of smells the city never seems to rid itself of. Rome is held in such high regard for its urban design and particularly sewars, but essentially, they laid a foundation for city pollution. No human was ever meant to be corralled the way they are in the city. Like horses enslaved on the steppes of Asia by the men destined to destroy matriarchy and take ownership of the world, people are leashed to this cement, the real estate, some man's buildings, and his dead-end corners of the maze.

If there's freedom in this city, it's only in the remnants of the counterculture mindset and the occasional breeze from the Pacific. The kids who inherited this way of thinking would rather share everything they have then fight.

Any restaurant on the avenue signed up for the Bezerkley subculture. Affectionately or not, everyone is served and there's always scraps in the dumpsters. Homeless of all persuasions can get fed well on the streets in the Bay Area, even in 1989 at the height of Republican baby boomer capitalism. Some establishments show their Bay Area pride, and this particular Ethiopian spot was beloved for hanging a Grateful Dead Steal Your Face poster on their wall, the universal symbol for a safe space for the kids. So close to the university, the beer flowed without question and no one behind the counter ever asked, 'Can I see your ID?'

Peter, Kyle, and Eddie ordered a pitcher because they only had enough money for one. In the middle of the Stealie on the wall, spitballs clung to the white 13-point bolt. A kind of ritual, the blotter paper spit wads were just another sign of reprieve from the outside world of checkbooks and expectations. Eat paper and spit it at the poster, hit the bullseye.

Inside his pocket, Peter felt a small bindle and took it out for further inspection. Sure enough, some powder was clinging to it, enough for him to split the paper in thirds. Waiting for beer, Peter chewed on the paper and shot a wallop of spit on it towards the poster. Kyle chewed with a big smile, "Tasty." Most likely to tar up his pitchers glove in the World Series, he hacked a jelly loogy at the poster. The paper stuffed in his biological adhesive, hit with a goo.

Famous last words are only called that because they have consequence. For Eddie, all the sucking he could muster made for a slick spit wad. Puckering up, his takes flight with precision. They all hit the mark, striking the Owsley bolt, a sweet reminder of the power of paper.

The pitcher came and went. Back out on the avenue, barely buzzing but enough to keep the edge off, Peter could make out Isabel walking towards them. Fishnets, miniskirt, combat boots and flight jacket, she was punk rock and Italian with a habit no different than anyone else in her scene.

"Hey Pete, you got a twenty?" she asked. He might have one, and often did, breaking up whatever's clever to make a dollar on the street. But he didn't put his hand in his pocket to investigate because she started to turn into a black rose. Her face flowering in a darkness, her mouth a pistil, and her hair disappearing into raven hued petals. Peter was scared. This was scary! He felt paranoid and looked around at the street. Isabel is a velvety black rose, and he feels high. Starting to really trip, an accordion called out. A street performer on the corner plays a psychedelic polka to Peter and he leaves his body.

Over Telegraph, he could see the busy corner and the dusk sink over the coastline. The rose grew smaller and smaller, the concrete jungle a speck from his bird's eye view. Higher and higher went his vantage.

Like a bolt from a storm, Peter shot back inside his body, the same way he left. Twenty feet down the road from the black rose, he sat up on the corner and sang at the top of his lungs. It was three, maybe four in the morning. No one was around, just Peter. Coherent and back in Berkeley, he got up and headed to Roachdale, the moniker for a cheap apartment with Redwoods and a hill in the back that dipped down and made for a nice spot to sleep. No one bothered the kids in the grassy nob, they could snooze in peace under the large trees. With his sleeping bag, Peter set out to take his rest on the empty spot. Relieved, he found a place and tucked inside the down cushioning.

On his back, he looked up at the stars. The hallucinations returned, and his mind drifted back into crystal conversation. He could see his dreadlocks were now buds, long marijuana colas. The planet underneath and around him was a forest, there was no more concrete. All the people are hanging out in tribes, together, in the tall redwood trees. A real Eden, he ruminates. There are waterfalls, and everyone swims up to them and eats the buds in their hair for sustenance and they get them high! It's wonderful, perfect for Peter because eating your hair buds keeps you high all the time.

He felt the heat. The sun, that stalwart blessing and curse, made its return. Peter woke in his sleeping bag. He swished around his mouth, it's full of grass! Straw-like strands of Bermuda grass flank his teeth. He ejects it bit by bit, spitting it out. Rubbing his eyes, he thought, 'what was last night?' Looking around, all the grass within arm's length is gone. Patches pulled out of the dirt! He was high with a stomach full of grass!

The next day, Peter made it over to People's Park and related his circumstances with some kids. They laugh and laugh, and Peter starts coughing. He coughs and coughs and out shoots a foxtail. "Oh, I had a scratch in my throat all day."

Quality Hotel

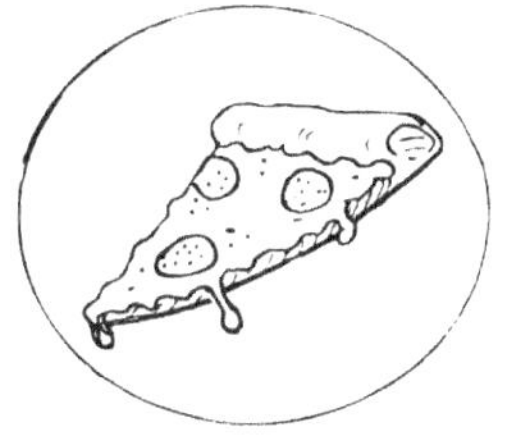

Nate and Ian met Dara and Lorena while getting pizza slices in Philly. They were in Little Jamaica and broke. But they scrounged up for a hotel room, and the foursome checked in.

Lorena pressed the buzzer on the door. A man talked through the speaker and told her it will be five bucks.

"For the night?"

"Oh. You want it for the night?"

"Yeah."

He mulled it over for a long pause, his cerebrum pushing at all walls. "Ten bucks?"

The hotel room was bleak and far from proper. But it would do for this one night. Dara immediately stripped the bed of its sheets, flipped the mattress over and threw down her sleeping bag on top.

"Want to watch a movie?" Ian asked the room.

"Yes, totally," Lorena agreed.

Nate opened the window and sat on the edge to smoke a cigarette. Downstairs, just below their room, a hooker was banging some guy. Her loud moaning broke through the paper-thin insulation. He lit his smoke and looked down, outside at the dirty street. 'Could be worse,' crosses his mind—then he notices a homeless dude mesmerized, staring up at the window of the hooker, and he's jacking off.

MSG vs. NYPD

"Hey, you want the end of this bottle?" Ernesto relayed to Rick. The rain was coming down, the streets were wet, and it was getting close to showtime. "You want to dose people with this bottle?"

"Yeah," Rick said and took the small plastic bottle.

A few minutes later, Rick was dosing a brother and behind his shoulder, a face popped up suddenly. "Hey, can I get some of that?" the voice inquired. Intuition kicked in and he threw the bottle out into the rain. Three undercover cops emerged like scum off the sidewalk and jumped Rick. Knees to the ribs, they pushed him up against the fence and yanked him over to their cop car.

"You piece of shit drug dealers!" one screamed at him.

"We're going to beat your head in so hard you're a real Deadhead," another one joked.

"Yeah, we're going to put your head on the subway tracks!" the next one spit out.

"We're going to push you into traffic and say you ran away from us!"

"No one will care, no one will miss you!"

"We're going to kill you!"

Hauled into the station, Rick was a wet dog, crumpled up from their beating. He couldn't believe these assholes dragged him all the way to the station.

"We're taking this shit upstairs," the pig started on him, "we're going to test it and charge you with homicide. Somebody died from this shit last night."

Rick was like, 'holy fuck.' How was he going to get out of this? But his mind started to wander. He realized he was just sitting there, and these assholes were screaming at him, but they never actually showed him they had the bottle. He put the pieces together, and knew they never found that bottle, because they never even looked for it. 'Bullshit,' he thought.

Feeling him up and down, a cop pulled off his money belt that was fastened around his waist. Inside his pocket, he had a pipe and his ticket to the show. But they were interested in his money belt and emptied it out onto the desk. There were no drugs, just a bunch of fake tickets Rick was making all day, taping together old stubs.

"We could just take these and tear them up!" one of them yelled. Rick knew they were full of shit. He had his real ticket in the pocket of his pants.

"A money belt, with no money," the other one said. "No money. You ain't got no money, tough time in New York City with no money," he laughed at Rick. He was getting fucked with hard. These pigs wanted to shame him, scare him, and just plain ruin his night.

The third cop came back from upstairs and presented Rick with a ticket for disorderly conduct, and they shoved him back outside into the rain.

He ran and ran and ran into a rainstorm, ducked into a bar door. It was Madison Square Garden. He ran into the show, not a drop on him, and they opened with *Jack Straw > Bertha*.

Later that night, the same three worthless degenerate cops snuck up on Ernesto outside a hotel and made him empty ten vials right onto the sidewalk in front of the hotel. They didn't do anything to him, just bullied their way through his stash.

The next morning, Ernesto and Rick were drinking coffee and smoking cigarettes, walking down the street and they saw the very same three NYPD officers. One of them sneered, “Hey, how’s it going?” as if he had a shred of authentic connection.

The brothers nodded, acknowledging their complete absence of humanity.

Finding Gerard

Wilshire Boulevard at Western is dirty deep city Ktown and on the southeast corner, the Wiltern shines like an ancient star cluster. In November of 1990, the Jerry Garcia Band arrived in this part of Los Angeles. A chilly night, inside it was a hot dance party, boiling hard with a *Run for the Roses* and an *Evangeline.*

In the lot behind the theater, a large chain grocery store shares a three-story concrete parking structure that all the kids park in and sell their wares. Patches, shirts, beers, balloons, it's all there.

Heads were packing up; the show was over, and some time had passed. Milling around with her last cigarette, Zen saw a small, cute, tiny puppy. She ran over to him, investigated his little face and picked him up. An adorable mutt, half beagle, half German shepherd, part wolf, he was a little cutie with floppy ears. No one was around, everyone split back on the road and this pup was going to be stranded. She was not going to let that happen.

Zen drove her van out of the parking garage with Fabian and Tai. The pup had no problem with this ride, he snuggled right up in some blankets and fell asleep.

Heading to San Francisco, they decided to name the pup Gerard. When they got to the city, Zen pulled into the Panhandle to finally get some sleep.

In the morning, she took Gerard for a walk. She wanted a smoke badly and saw a couple brothers down the street leaning against a school bus she could bum one from. As she walked up with Gerard, one of the guys had a moment of instant recognition.

"Hey, I've seen this little cutie before," the younger one said after he handed her the smoke.

"Yeah?"

These brothers didn't say anything but smiled. "He likes you, though," the older guy replied. She took a hit and they all watched Gerard go do his duty on the grass.

"Hey, man, is this your dog?" Zen asked this old man.

"Ah, well, he's yours. Keep him, his name is Kenobi."

Back at the van, Zen climbed in holding Gerard. Tai was rolling a fatty.

"His name is Kenobi," she reported. "But I think that's more of a middle name, don't you?"

"Yeah," Tai said.

"Well, then his full name is, Gerard Kenobi Red Carpet Treatment Love Puppy."

Losing it All in New Mexico

That winter, some kids got up enough cash to get themselves off Telegraph and on tour. Hank traded his Toyota Celica for a Chevy Van and these marauders piled in after the Oakland shows on the road to Arizona. The scene at Compton Terrace was fun, they raged the shows and camped nearby hassle-free. Hustling just enough cash to get to the next shows in Colorado, Hank drove his van to Albuquerque and then up through Santa Fe.

Jessica, Patricia, Garrett, Rodney, Lou and Hank had never been through this part of the country. They marveled at the changes in landscape. The flat desert land turned into slanted mountains, with peaks shooting up in the direction of Taos. Super green, big pines appeared in the dry mountainy areas. Highway 40 to the 25 is the road to McNichols in Denver, and Hank decided to pull off in Santa Fe. With some dollars in their pockets, albeit still pretty broke, the kids set out to spare change and wander the streets of the small, charming colonial town.

Like every small, "charming" colonial town there's a square in the center of Santa Fe. Little art galleries and shops dot the periphery. Local Indigenous folks sit outside at tables making jewelry and adobe houses spread out from the interior. Santa Fe is an area taken and colonized by the Spanish, named 'Holy Faith' in their language. It's a violent chapter for the Tewa and Navajo, and all the ancestors who lived in the area for thousands of years before any churches or art galleries stole land and took ownership.

The community of wealthy hippies and baby boomers are delighted by Hank and the others presence. Like a welcome change of pace, they're reminded what freedom looks like when dreadlocked nature loving Deadheads pass through town. Kids taking a stand, not paying taxes, living by their own rules. Another batch of kids on tour are posted up in a Subaru nearby. Friendly with Hank and the crew, they have herb for sale and hope to get on the road to Colorado soon, so Hank arranges a trade for a kind ounce of weed.

Jessica and Garrett spare change on an adjacent vein of the square and come up like crazy, getting a slew of twenties from passersby. On another corner, Patricia is handed a hundy, not once, but twice! The rich hippies are happy to see them and want to help these poor angels get to their next destination. But after a couple hours, an irate over privileged square shopkeeper grows tired of watching them hustle. A stain on his pleasant and well carved out existence, he simply doesn't want to look at kids with dirty clothes, natty hair, and smiles. He tolerates the local tribespeople because they bring a special mood and historical context for tourists, but these grungy hippie kids had no business here.

"Mike, you know, I've been patient, but these dirty hippies just will not leave the square. There were two carloads of 'em, and I waited, and one finally skedaddled but the other ones are still roaming free, begging and bothering every soul in proximity," he spoke into the telephone to the local authorities, most likely inbred and white for sure. Only a couple token Mexican Americans were to be had on this police force in 1990.

Kicked off the square not twenty minutes later, Hank and the kids rounded up for a night at a motel. Better off with more in their wallets, they smoked some weed, ate a pizza and drifted to sleep. The next morning, they drove on to Taos. All kinds of Deadheads were posted up on the highway, all on their way to Denver, the vibe was alive. Rodney and Lou hopped in another ride and left the guys with Patricia and Jessica. By this time, they had about eighty bucks left between them, some food, a full tank of gas and a little bit of the ounce left. Good shape. They catch some z's in the van and head out of the dreamy sand rust colored town on a beautiful drive through tall green trees. This scenery is so new and magical, they can't take their eyes away from the windows, looking and dreaming.

Garrett holes a pipe out of a carrot with a screwdriver and they puff. The sun comes up and the trees cast shade around the corners on the highway. Just enough gray area to hide a patch of ice on this December morning. Taking a hit off the carrot pipe, Hank does not see that patch of ice coming.

He drives the van around the corner, slides straight through the ice, hits a sign and lands in a bank off the road. Trying to back it out, the van is stuck on the sign. With no tools, Garrett can't get the sign to budge, the bolt is jammed into the front of the van grill.

A truck drives by and stops. Kevin, a local redneck gearhead, wants to come to the rescue. Their disturbance could cause another one and he knows all about that, been stuck on the highway behind looky-loo's too many times to count on the 25. Inspecting the mishap, he speculates to Hank, "If you take the bolt out, I can pull you right out."

"I don't have any tools, I have no idea how I can get that thing off," Hank reasons.

"I don't know then," Kevin sighs to himself. But around the corner comes a tow truck, a godsend in the mountains.

Jake, another redneck on the road, leans out of the window intrigued and pulls over to the side. Hank feels a glimmer of possibility and tells him, "Look, if you can take that bolt off, he is going to try and pull us out. It could work. All I have is eighty bucks, I'll give it to you if you can help us." Jake sizes it all up. He's got the upper hand, and he knows it.

"I'm going to try it anyway, lemme just hook the truck up." Hank shakes his head, but why not let him try? Jake latches on to the van, and gives the gas a go a few times, but there's no pull. That bolt has got it locked up real hard, the van is not going anywhere. "Well, I tried for ya. That'll be eighty bucks," he says to Hank.

"Dude, you gotta take the bolt off. I told you."

"Eighty bucks."

"Man, I asked you to help get the bolt off and you went about on your own without checking out how it's stuck," Hank protests. Within moments, as if the early morning melt pulled the wool off some state trooper's dense cavity of a brain, around the corner comes New Mexico's finest state highway patrol. The old guard pulls up, swift and inefficient as ever. Hank senses his judgement before the man even gets out of his patrol car but he's going to give him the truth.

"Officer, we slid off the ice and the van is stuck to that bolt on the sign. This tow truck pulled in and said he'd take off the bolt for eighty bucks, but he didn't listen. He just pulled up his hitch and of course, can't pull us out. He's trying to extort all my cash from me."

"You sayin' my brother-in-law is lying?" the pig retorts. This is not the first time this charade has been acted out on the side of Highway 40 and won't be the last until the land is given back to the Tewa once and for all. Property is theft, and these assholes only know what's theirs. The kids waited on the side of the road while the cop talked to Jake, his scheming brother-in-law, hope for any help crushed. Jake slides underneath the van and takes off the bolt. The pig lays down his plan, "Get your shit out of the van, you're all coming with me." Damned if they do, the kids pull their backpacks out and reluctantly get into the patrol car. Is this their end? Will it be a firing squad in the middle of this cursed colonized land?

Right as Hank steps in, Jake pulls his shoulder back. "Where's my eighty dollars?" Hank looked over at the cop, as if.

"I believe he took that bolt off, best pay the man for his services. You kids are way out here, you sure needed his help. You're lucky, aren't you?" He fingered his baton. Aggression his one and only muse. Hank wants to run but there's nowhere except off the side of the mountain, into the thicket of pines.

"Motherfucker," Hank hands over the cash, the last they have.

"What?" the cop questions. "Did you say, thank you?"

"Thank you kindly," Hank says with a sarcastic smile.

Patricia leans forward and, in his ear, reminds him, "Karma is his bitch." The cop eyes her unsteadily. She leans back and beams another sarcastic smile at him.

Jake pulls the van out of the ice and tows it south back towards Taos. The patrol car turns in the opposite direction, north down the cold road.

Dusk lingered down the highway and darkness seized the last of the day. The patrol car drops the kids off at an intersection with a small country store. Cornflake sized snowflakes drop, and Patricia sticks out her thumb. She looks for the magic in this stroke of deception. Another reason to never give in to the system, to be a 'civilian' with no guarantees, no protection, and certainly zero loyalty. Humans? Or another race that raped ours? She wished she could see the answer clearly but, in her heart, she knew the 'civilized' are wrong. It was probably devolution. A truck pulls over and the kids load up in the back of the pickup, the lift back to Taos a warm gesture in the freezing cold.

Back in town, the girls scout for a church. The last house that can help them often carried hotel vouchers for the weary and destitute. Patricia and Jessica play that game, and the men hunt down more cash. Spare-changing in the plaza, there is a beacon of hope. Rich hippies continued to feel some accountability and connection to their own species, thankfully. The guys square up on one hundred and twenty-five dollars.

"We got one!" Patricia announces. The crew reunited, damaged but not beyond repair.

"Shit, let's go get some alcohol," Garrett demands.

Inside the liquor store, Hank makes a solid friend out of the cashier. Two cases of beer and a couple bottles of Boone's Farm, the man takes their cash and grins at the ladies. Garrett fishes through the pockets of his jacket and finds a miracle.

"Dude, I got a couple roaches!"

"Jah Rastafari!" Jessica belts out. A good laugh sets in; their faces soften.

"Oh, it's on," Hank agrees.

The tiny motel accepted their voucher and Jessica returns with the key to the corner room. "He took one look at me and gave us the farthest room, what a yanker."

"We clean up nicely, his loss," Garrett proclaims.

"Oh, this is fancy," she says when they open the room. Beige walls, cheap art bolted to the wall, and two double beds with coin massage capabilities.

Hank laughs, "I'm getting as shitfaced as this room." He breaks open the case of beer and the girls crack open the Boone's Farm. Garrett turns on the TV to a late night old black and white movie.

"Is this *Casablanca*?"

"No way, man. This is a pirate movie," Hank specifies.

Jessica studies it and says, "It's *The Count of Monte Cristo*, I've seen this before. At my grandparents, they love this movie."

Garrett lights the roach, and they finally find a reset back to normality.

"Fuck yes, everything is going to be alright," Hank says, hitting the weed hard.

Two hours later, a perfectly stacked beer pyramid adorns the stained coffee table. The law may have stolen from the kids and abandoned them in the cold, but the human desire to conquer persists. Weed lingers in the air, and Hank and Patricia make out sloppily, barely hanging onto their bed. Jessica and Garrett are buck naked rolling around on theirs until the mattress slides off the squeaky old metal frame, dumping them on the hard thin layer of carpet that pretty much feels like cement.

Roughly an hour after that, the couples are passed out. The door bursts open! The disheveled preacher who graciously gifted the motel voucher wanted his revenge!

When the light flips on, Garrett flips out. He pulls on his clothes and Jessica slides hers on under the covers. "Don't watch me!" she yells at the clergyman. He turns around and runs out, bothered, ashamed, and clearly too nosy.

"Fuck, we better jam," Hank admits. "What if he calls the cops?"

"Generosity their ass," Jessica slams.

Out on the miserable street again, the snow falls with no sign of letting up. "Fuck, what the hell, man," Hank complains. Their breath clouds out in front of their faces, puffy and thick in the freezing weather.

"We're never going to get a ride right now," Jessica sighs.

"I don't know about making it to Colorado, it's fucking cold, " Garrett adds, "going through the mountains doesn't sound like a good idea."

"And we're not going to make it to the show in time," Hank confesses.

"Let's just hitch back to Cali," Patricia reasons. "We have to split up, we have a better chance in pairs."

"Oh, this sucks," Garrett whines, "she's right." He kisses Jessica and hugs her tightly.

Patricia and Hank embrace. "See you later," she winks.

"Yep, good luck," he winks back.

Hank and Garrett walk along the highway. Hopeful but extremely cautious of any headlights that pass, a small Toyota pickup pulls over. Two local indigenous guys wave, and the driver motions to the back of the truck.

"He won't even roll down his window," Hank says.

"Yeah, it's way too cold." Garrett jumps in the back—into six inches of snow. "Oh, fuck, man."

"I hope he drives fast."

The guys hold on to the sides of the old truck and rest their laurels on the fresh powder. Not the time to make a choice, just the time to get the hell out before another Highway Patrolman wants to "help." Tortured by the wins and losses of the trip to Denver, now their thick corduroy pants were wet. Barely recovered from the hotel scene, there was magic in the snowfall. Cynicism and good old-fashioned survival help form smiles on their faces as the shitty road bumped below.

Hank leaned his head back against the truck rear window and remembered fixing the tape cassette player in the van when he bought it. There was an old tape jammed in it and on the road to Tempe, he managed to pull it out, tape spaghetti all over the front console. But the machine still worked, and Jessica had her first show tape to play, which she carried everywhere. Hartford '88 had paved the road for the devoted kids happy and high on tour.

A thud against the window shook him from the daydream. He looks over and Garrett's eyes are wide open, not much could get him to shut down now. Any southern Florida boy would be challenged by this weather.

The truck pulls off the highway, and at least two hours have passed because the snow is higher no matter how much they kicked out away from them when they climbed into the bed. The truck stops and honks. Inside the driver throws them up a peace sign and points to the street.

"Where the fuck are we?" Hank wonders.

"Like I know? Let's find somewhere warm."

"It must be 5 a.m., when's the sun going to come up?"

"It will."

"Well, yeah, cops can't take that away."

They set out on the sidewalk and a few store windows down the block, they figure out they're in Albuquerque but all they really see is darkness.

"So?" Garrett questions.

"We need another ride."

They walk through town, following the highway, not too far from the only lifeline they may have back to California. It's clean, but dismal and empty.

"Let's just get to the next onramp," Hank suggests. Every step is crispy, their bones frosty. Fifteen minutes later, they see the open highway again. "That's it, we need to be there."

Pacing, sitting, whistling, the guys stare down the quiet entrance to Highway 40. A faint light emerges in the horizon. "Well, I'll be, is that the sun?"

"I don't even know what the hell you're talking about. I can't feel my heart beating, I'm sure there's nothing that will save us now."

"Shut the fuck up, Garrett, that's the goddamn sun."

"That lucky old sun."

"Look!" Hank stammers.

A tiny Toyota pickup truck with an old camper shell pulls over. Hank can't make out the driver, but she actually gets out of the cab, in the cold.

"Hey, you need a ride?"

"Yes," Hank says and moves closer. Her complexion stood out, a chilling faint whiteness adjusting to the temperature. "Wait, I know you."

"You do?"

"Yeah."

She takes a closer look at him.

"Leah?"

"Yeah, Hank? What the fuck are you doing out here?"

"You know Garrett?"

"Hey, brother," she offers kindly.

"Hi. You got room for us?"

"Of course. Hop in. The heater works, it's not the best but it helps." She offers them the lift graciously.

Hank leans into Garrett, "Dude, I know her from Berkeley. She's a Rasta chick, super low key."

"Fuck, thank god."

"You guys got any money? I'm broke, been hustling gas to get back west," she confides.

"No, we got ripped off by the cops," Hank informs her. "They stole my van and took all our cash in Taos."

"No way. Fucking pigs, that sucks. Your van?"

"Yeah, straight up gaffled."

"Let's get going," she says.

The truck hit the highway and they spare changed for gas at every station on the way. That night Leah parked in a rest stop, and they all spooned in the camper shell. Warm, safe, and together.

The Great Dane Escape

Wandering the streets at dawn, the bay was wrought from celebration. As the sun peeked its way into everyone's next peak, the new year already had its grip. And it was a new day, another day in the shitty.

They'd been up all night. The meandering wanted meaning. Sean wondered what they were going to do. No one was hungry, no one needed anything. Everything was in its right place, so they decided to see what the youngsters were doing.

"We're at the Sleepy Inn. Come through, we got a tank," Daniel said through the payphone. "Dude, bring balloons, yeah?"

Sean and Eli drove across town to the hotel. It was quiet, the wee hours still wee. Inside the moderately priced cheap hotel, the hallway is practically serene. Sean and Eli exchange glances, surprised at how on the level it all seems so far. Quite frankly, they weren't even sure they were in the right place. But they found the room and Sean knocked on the door.

A wall of sound and cloud of marijuana smoke came out as the door opened. A small dog runs up to say hello. The room was packed, there are like a dozen teenagers and surely at least one eighteen-year-old, who booked the room. They've been raging all night in this two-bed ensemble with a desk, after all, it was a morning as good as any to write a list of intentions for the new year of the Lord. The Bible in fact had already been torched and pages were torn out to make paper airplanes that were scattered around from a previous episode of *Kids Wasted in a Hotel Room with Jesus.* Sean handed the small bag of balloons he brought over to Daniel and the kids clapped and snapped fingers in grateful delight.

Gabriel was in the chair at the desk, spinning around in circles. 'Wow, this is a scene,' Sean thought. He made his way to a corner and tucked in, game to watch it all go down. There were a dozen kids in the middle of the room, and Gabriel just spinning in the chair holding a fatty in one hand and a hotel trashcan garbage bag full of nitrous in the other, because they've been using these garbage bags in lieu of balloons. Sean watches him spin and spin, and somehow the fatty touches the garbage bag and everyone learned something new on that new year day: nitrous is flammable. The garbage bag balloon explodes, the top blows off the plastic and burns all the way around in a circle and on the edges. All the melted plastic drips into the cone that has been created and burns very quickly.

"What happened?" one kid says. They all watch the insanity, but Gabriel is in the wah wah wah zone and unaware. Sean sees the molten plastic moving closer and closer towards his hand. He leans in and reaches over the top and delicately slides it out of Gabriel's hand, twisting the bag to capture the molten plastic but drops of it fly around going "poof, poof, poof." All the little pieces of plastic go everywhere and burn things all over the room—including the carpet!

Sean nabs most of it and guides it into the actual trash can, saving Gabriel's hand from utter destruction. But several spots on the carpet are smoking and the smoke alarm is triggered. All the kids scramble, they need to get the hell out fast! One kid picks up the dog by the door and sneaks out quickly. No dogs were allowed in the first place. Sean and Eli crawl towards the front door, it was a good time to go. They pass a majestic Great Dane emerging from the side of one of the beds. A couple kids direct her towards the balcony, and in a carefully constructed plan, one of them jumps down to the ground level outside and the others lift the enormous dog over the cheap iron rail.

Guns of Lower Haight

Haight Street was crazy. An average day could have a mellow vibe for the most part, but there were no average days on the Haight. If the sun was shining, the neighborhood put off a strong vibration. It was somewhere people could just be, could score drugs, and could watch other people just be and score drugs.

After a night at the Days Inn in Oakland, Jeremiah and Oscar caught the BART back into the city and got off at Civic Center. They walked a ways to lower Haight to catch the bus back up and start hustling weed. Weed was expensive, forty-eight hundred for a pound translated to four hundred an ounce all the way up. Jeremiah and Oscar would often buy a pound, or get it on the front, and break it down to twelve to sixteen bags and sell them for forty to sixty dollars each, depending on the custy. Was there a relationship? Did they seem cool? Do they look like cash money? There were many ways to vet a custy before you even heard a word out of their mouth. Most of the time it was sixty an eighth to the city custies and even tourists who maybe wanted to have the experience of buying weed on Haight Street, akin to getting a balloon at a carnival. If the street was flooded, the bags might go for forty-five.

They could sell an ounce or two a day like that, possibly even a quarter pound. You play the prices and break it up and they could each make at least two hundred a day and just chill skateboarding. At 4:20 p.m. they'd go to 710 Ashbury and smoke weed with the kids on the sidewalk outside. Everyone heard the people that owned the house hated that, but what do they expect buying a house that was an important intersection for the counterculture music scene of the sixties? Seems weird to want that connection and hate the neighborhood kids for smoking weed there. Kids used to joke about it. The residents could come outside and get stoned for free every day at 4:20 and charge for tours, but they never made nice with the kids outside.

Walking to the bus stop on lower Haight, an Oldsmobile had the trunk open. Jeremiah and Oscar glanced over and saw a dude selling military issue .45's in little wooden crates for a hundred bucks each. Jeremiah's head ignited. 'This is bad,' he thought, 'I'm swinging bags of weed down the street and this dude's slinging' .45's right here. Some motherfuckers gonna come at me with a 45.'

A week or so later, all the kids on the Haight heard about these three guys robbing people.

Jeremiah only carried one bag with him on the street. He stashed the rest, that way if he ever got caught, it's only possession. More than one bag is possession with the intent to sell. He usually kept the bag in his sleeve because anyone looking would check his pockets and if they made him put his hands up against a wall or some other surface, his hands were right there on point, but the weed was up his sleeve out of sight. All the kids kept bags in their sleeves, it was the best hiding spot.

Skating around the panhandle that afternoon, a man approached Jeremiah and Oscar for an eighth. Jeremiah sat down on a bench with the dude to make the deal. He talked to him for a moment about the price and noticed three dudes come out from behind the trees and beeline right for them. One of the dudes had a gun and straight up put the .45 to his Jeremiah's head and told him swiftly, "Empty your pockets."

He had around a thousand dollars in his pocket, but in those days the kids wore baggy pants, and the pockets were deep and large. He reaches in and pulls out everything but the cash and throws it on the ground.

"That's all I got," he says.

"Where's the money?"

"He didn't give me the money yet."

Dude takes the bag of weed and the man's money from him. He points the gun at Oscar, and he pulls out everything from his pockets, including a wad of cash, and gives it him. Somewhat satisfied, the gunman splits with his crew.

Walking back up the corner, Jeremiah grills Oscar, "What did you give them? All your everything?"

"Yeah."

"Fuck man, I threw everything out, but my money and he put a .45 right up to my head." Oscar is pissed! He skates off in another direction to blow off steam on every cement bank he can manage.

Jeremiah walks back up on Haight and sees a guy take off running, right next to his friends Marcus and Kevin. Something just went down for sure, and this guy took off, so Jeremiah runs after him. The man turns the corner and goes up the street. It's all uphill but Jeremiah chases after him, he's about a block and a half behind and gaining speed. In the distance, a ways behind him, back towards the street, he hears faintly, "Jeremiah, he's got a gun!"

The man gets his bearings and looks back. Jeremiah is sure enough right on his tail. BAP BAP BAP goes the gun, and bullets fly past Jeremiah! He jumps behind a car. BAP BAP BAP, bullets hit the car and ricochet. He stays put and pushes himself as far down as he can, almost underneath the car. The bullets stop.

"Hey! Jeremiah, hey!" Marcus calls out to him. "Get over here, man!"

He runs back down to the street. The man tried to gaffle Marcus earlier and Kevin grabbed him, but he pulled out his .45, shot them both and took off running.

At the hospital, the doctors could not remove the bullet from Marcus, but he lived. After he got out of the hospital, he split the

Haight to grow and sell bags to rich kids in a small college town over a hundred miles away.

RITA

Not a bad day, not an exceptional day, but it was a decent day hustling herb, so Andrew and Danielle were up on Haight Street drinking beers. A few other swinger kids lingered, and Rita was in prime form, heckling and hugging anyone she wanted to fuck with. Rita was an old schooler, a Haight Street elder to this generation of kids, and she either knew you, or she was damn well going to know you. And if you were a guy, she was going to take ownership—and you'd have to learn to laugh about it.

420 came and went, and everyone was getting schwilly. Fresh blood, Tim had never hung on Haight before. Out from the east coast for the Oakland run, he was living the California sunshine daydream. His pockets had a jar of quality headstash and glass, and he had a chill place to stay in the Sunset with a crew of east coast high rollers. He was on his hero's journey, the integral coming of age trip to San Francisco: puffing at 710 Ashbury, skating the panhandle, kicking back on Haight Street, and if he's really up for it, he'll end up on Jones and Eddy chasing one of the many dragons the city has to offer.

Rita tied one on and every time she needed another Tim took good care of her. It felt like a proper hazing, he knew she was to be respected but he had no idea what he was getting into. She was a legend, thick with the family and a specific crew that no one messed with. You either knew or you didn't, and if you didn't, you were a custy.

Andrew lit the wrong end of a smoke; it was time for Danielle to drag him away. She was plenty saucy herself and they needed to get across the bay to a cheap hotel for the night.

"Sock 'em up!" Rita screamed at them when they left, her arm locked in a solid grip on Tim, she was ready for the next beer.

"You gotta let go, Rita. I'll be right back, I got you, girl."

"Yeah, you sure do. You better!" She let him go and reached over to kiss his cheek, but he moved fast, he was wising up, but he was well on the way to shitface drunk.

The next morning, Danielle and Andrew were back and getting coffee in McDonald's by the park. Not too hazy, they find a chill spot in the panhandle to smoke a joint and get rid of some bags. Puffing a fatty, the coffee kicks in, and they light cigarettes. The hippie speedball comes on and Rita pops out of the sandbox behind them!

"What the hell, Rita, we're up in your bedroom," Andrew joked.

Rita spit, coughed up some more and spit again. Awakened, the legend could feel her blood flow, it was a brand-new day in the shitty. Stretching her short arms out, she pulled on her crocheted beanie. Next to her, sand slips away like the time in an hourglass, and Tim emerges. Tore up from the floor up, he slept with Rita all night!

"Hey man, get a good night's rest?" Andrew can't help himself. Tim looks around, he wants to get his bearings straight but his head pounds.

"What happened? Where are we?"

"Hey honey, yeah, we got drunk last night, and then we started making out, we started kissing," she recounts.

"Haha haha!!" Danielle blurts out.

"Yeah, man, you're in love."

"Oh, you're gonna have my baby! He's my boyfriend, right Danielle?"

"Yaup, Rita, that's the way we do it! It's the sand trap!"

"Ohhhh, ha ha ha ha! Come here honey, lay one on me," Rita puckers up and moves in even closer, adjusting her weight in the dirty sand.

“Ha ha ha! Haight Street honies caught kissing!” Andrew says.

“Oh yeah, come on, come here, boy,” she tells Tim, but he tumbles out of the sandbox as quickly as his baggy ass corduroy’s filled with sand will let him.

“Where you going, Tim? Long way home, kid!” Danielle roasts him.

He stumbled up on to his two feet and ran off so fast, someone might’ve thought he was getting chased by the pigs.

“Bye sweetie, see you soon!” Rita screamed.

No one ever saw Tim on the Haight again.

The War Field

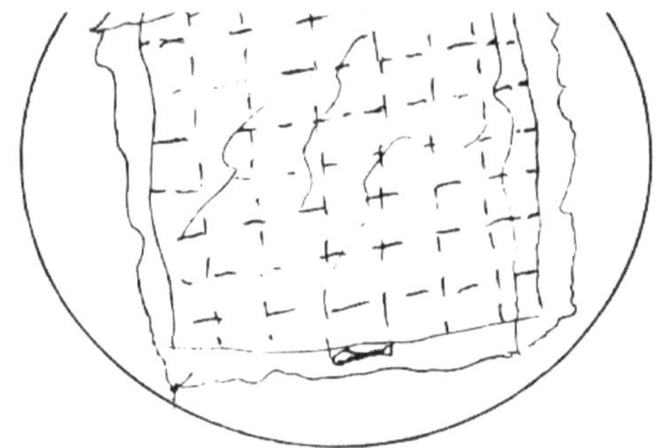

At the top of the Haight, there was a bowling alley with a bar and a few pool tables. On the way to see Jerry Garcia Band play the Warfield, Jack and Stan put away some beers and whined about their hustle. Stressed for cash, they both could've had a better day to finance the party tonight but there's nothing else to be done now. Neither of them wanted to put more effort in on the street before the show so here they are drinking up a couple pitchers until it's time take a bus down to Market Street.

"Yeah, I still got a quarter, fuck man," Stan bitched.

"Shut up. Quit complaining."

"Thank for the beers is all I'm saying'."

"Comes around."

"Dude I can't wait, the show's gonna be sick."

Leaving the bowling alley through the parking lot, it was a pleasant early evening with the bay breeze meandering like a partner on the boulevard. Out of nowhere, but not really because it's the city after all, a disturbed man straight runs up on them! He's got his hand under his shorts like he's got a pistol in his pants waistline and charges up into Jack's face, "What's up with the Rodney King verdict?"

Jack mutters back, "I don't even know who that is."

The disturbed man kept on, "What's up with that?" He insists Jack knows but he keeps telling him he has no idea who Rodney King is. Stan is completely puzzled and ready to throw down if this kook sets to rob them. But Matt skates up and explains that the police in L.A. beat up Rodney King and the verdict just came down and it must not be good.

"Remember, the black guy who got beat up by the cops last year?"

"Ohhh, yeah," Jack says.

"Best be on your toes," Matt advises.

The brothers finally recall who Rodney King is. It's not surprising they didn't remember right away. They are white hippie kids with dreadlocks selling bags of weed on the streets of San Francisco unplugged, making ends to survive supplying plant medicine to people who haven't been totally brainwashed by the war on drugs or Jesus. Why would King's case affect them now, miles away? Or, conversely, why would it not? King was chumped by potentially the most racist branch of pigs in California, the LAPD Foothill Division. The case was tried in Simi Valley, potentially the most racist court in California. The dice were loaded from the get-go, nothing new in good ol' United States.

On Market Street, getting up to the Warfield, the breeze moves through again, wishing it could clean up the nonsense in the air. A few rabid men run past Jack and Stan with bloodied hands carrying loads of gold jewelry. Necklaces, bracelets, and bolos dripping from the stranglehold of angry opportunists.

Jack and Stan charge up the pavement to get a reading on the mayhem and sure enough a jewelry store window is broken. Glass shines on the asphalt, the store is straight fucked up. SFPD is on the scene, civilians looted the store, smashed the windows, and got away with it all in the name of civil unrest. Anarchy in revolt against white American privilege. Again. The L.A. police officers were not convicted for their abuse. Again, the institution proved to be racist, constructed for the safety of whitey. Rape the local pawn shop or Bert's Diamonds to cause ruckus and force change. Somewhere a mayor smiles and a police chief is eating prime rib with a Budweiser.

It was easy to get a ticket and duck into the show that night. They closed the first set with *Let's Spend the Night Together.*

"I want to give you a little update about what's going on outside. First off, what I'd like to say is that, inside I think we have the only safe and sane place on Market Street. But outside things are a little different. Since you've all come in and the music has started, the mayor has declared a curfew on the city. So, we've talked to the police department, we've said, listen we have two thousand people having a good time, we don't want to send them home yet. So, they agreed with us but it's really important that we all work together to make this work tonight, because I know we have the ability to do it. Let me give you a little information, BART is still running, but they've closed the Embarcadero, Montgomery, Powell, and Civic Center stations. I would say that those of you coming on BART, the closest station is 16th Street, which is way away and I would suggest not trying to get there on your own, if there's a large group of you, like ten or twenty people want to make the trek, that might work, but a couple people, you might have trouble. Secondly, there's a lot of people who came in cars tonight, they probably have a seat or two open in their car so during intermission now's the time to do a little networking, find the person that's going to your town, get yourself a ride, those of you that have a seat, find somebody that needs a ride. We're all here together. We can make this work if we're just all here together. When everything ends and you still don't have a ride home, don't go out walking on the street alone. Stay here, walk up to the front, we'll try to work something out for you, one way or another."

—David Graham, onstage during intermission, April 30, 1992

Several more beers later, Jack had an idea.

"Maybe we could make some money?" he busts.

"I need some fucking money," Stan replied.

Their beat-up skate shoes hit the cement outside and scrambled across the street. A busted-up window on a Miller's Outpost now served as the door. Scooting his way in past some other looters, Jack grabbed a stack of blue jeans. His friend Franklin left the show too and had parked his VW bus nearby, so he stashed them in there.

Shards of glass cracked and smashed in every direction. An electronics store nearby lost its front window display, and someone wasn't doing a good job stepping over pieces to get a hold of a color TV.

The guys looked at each other and raced up to the store. Stan b-lined for some new DVD players in boxes stacked in storage below a display. DVD players! State of the art, he grabs two and heads back to the VW. Jack lifts one and runs. They load them in, and Jack looks back, "What do you think?"

Stan's eager. "Let's go see." The electronics store had more to offer. The guys ran off with two more DVD players each, grinning. Stan locked himself in the bus with Franklin. The plan was to head down to Isla Vista after the shows and rage herb on the college kids.

"Let's meet up at Greyhound and crash," Jack suggested.

"Yeah, man, see you there," Franklin said. He waved goodbye and started up the bus.

Jack headed back towards the Warfield to meet Debby. She was posted up lighting a smoke with some sisters and waved him over. "Hey, man, it's fucking nuts out here."

"Rodney King," one of the sisters reminds. "Fuck those pigs."

Some rando guy walks up to Jack and inquires, "You have any L, man, any paper?" Jack sizes him up. He's never seen him before and he looks about forty years old, with khakis and a button up tie-dyed collared shirt. His stylist gave him the hard undercover cop look.

In the already way too fucking sketchy air, Jack's instinct is 'fuck this guy' but one of the sisters, Cindy catches on. Jack asks quietly, "Hey, any of you know this guy? 'Cause he looks like a cop to me."

Cindy slyly nods, "he's cool, he knows Cameron and his crew. I seen him with them."

"Aha," Jack mulls it over for a beat. "Okay, man, let's go."

"My friend has his van parked right around the corner," the dude beams, happy to assist how he can. Typical custy.

Up Taylor Street, next to the Warfield, the dude's 80's Vanagon bus is parked, indifferent to the melee. Jack feels in his pocket for the paper, wrapped in cellophane. He pulls it out discreetly as he walks to the bus and tears off a chunk of the sheet, the rest was going to Isla Vista. Those college kids paid hands over fist for acid. It was an easy hustle down there, especially during Halloween. Always prepare.

The bus doors swing open and some guy startles Jack as he pokes his head out. "You good?"

"Yeah," Jack says. The custy hands him cash and Jack counts a hundred. "Here you go, have fun, man." He presses it into the man's palm and a cop car pulls up on the other side of the bus! 'Holy shit,' Jack thinks. "What the fuck?"

Two cops jump out of the car and run around both sides of the Vanagon. The custy freezes, he can't even compute what's happening. Jack takes off running. He thrusts his hand in his pocket and puts the rest of the paper wrapped in cellophane in his mouth. Safe keeping.

In the distance, behind him, that chilly bay breeze flies through and a voice cut above it, "What's he running for?" Amused and stupid, the cop watches Jack kick up dust. He looks back and the other cop is arresting a crack head that was right next to the Vanagon.

No one noticed the poor man selling crack rocks to some tweaker, they're off Market after all, but the cops apparently noticed and even in the middle of a riot they want to haul a man off the street for making a dollar. How did Jack miss them? They were right behind him.

The two cops were fat and skinny and the skinny one put the cuffs on the dealer. "I don't know, I got him. You go get him," he ordered his sidekick.

The fat man scampered up the sidewalk after Jack who is already thinking about where he can spit out the cellophane. Lean and fast from skating, Jack outruns this fat cop easy, up a few blocks. He feels a joint in his pocket, and tosses it, just in case. Turning the corner, he's about to spit out the cellophane in his hand. Cutting left, Jack runs right in the police station! Pigs are everywhere, congregating over their jarhead roles in the riot and planning for the disheveled looters they manhandled off the street. They grab him easy and search him. 'Shit,' he has one little mushroom cap in his pocket for the ride down to Isla Vista. Pigs fucking found it.

The fat cop catches up finally, worn out and pissed off. Huffing and puffing, he's like, "Are you kidding me? You cuffed him without me? Goddamn idiot over here." He slams Jack up against the wall and the car and twists him around. They face each other. The mean angry pig yanks on Jack's beard and pulls it around and puts it over his shoulder and pulls him into the station. He's hijacked on his tippy toes in handcuffs.

The police station has at least a hundred people inside. It's packed with crazy riot energy, weirdos squirming, humans in revolt, tagged and caged. Jack is yanked inside, and the cop stands him up at attention once he can find an audience. "Hey, hey! Everyone quiet. Now!" The entire room freezes and looks up at him, with Jack enslaved. The cop tightens his hold in full performance and delivers, "Everyone, this is dumbest hippie in San Francisco, we weren't even after him and he takes off running straight to the police station."

Everyone laughs and points at him. Jack has like one hundred and eighty hits of acid in his mouth in cellophane. He gets handcuffed to a bench and begins to chew it as he sits down next to a large man. Chewing and chewing, it doesn't go down his throat and he starts to turn blue, and the big man says, "Hey dude, you're turning blue man, you want me to yell for the police officers?"

Jack muffles, "Mrrrrrmrrr," and gulp, he swallows it down. Not getting that charge. A skinny cop with a long nose takes him to a holding cell and gives him a cot and a corner. Resting, his body shut down slowly and he drifted off to sleep. Always time for a nap. He woke up and felt kind of high but remembered what was going on. He's moved to another holding cell. The only thing left to do is try to pay attention. But he's high. Lying down on a cot again, his body turns off. He wakes up the next day. When he looks around, he realizes he's in 850 Bryant and high as a kite. The linoleum floor speaks to him, "A-B-C-1-2-3-Grateful Dead!" Jack stares at it forever until a man breaks through to his only level left for human communication.

This man exclaims, "Move your fucking cot so we can get our fucking trays!" Jack is lying on the cot, staring at the floor, and his cot is blocking the door this man needs to get through along with a line of inmates behind him waiting to get their trays. He's staring at the floor but gets up and picks up his cot. He finds a bunk and places it there. All he can do is get a tray, so he turns around with it and runs into a Samoan dude who takes his tray away from him immediately.

He explains, "No one's stealing no one's tray in here." What is even happening, Jack can't comprehend, so he puts two and two together and grabs his own spork from the bottom end. With his hand on the tray, he looks at the dude in the eyes. A madman, high as a kite with a spork. He went back to the cot and laid down. Perhaps someone spoke to him, but he forgot what the first word of their sentence was, his mind expanding rapidly.

It was maybe one gram of mushrooms. They wouldn't keep him long. He knew that much somewhere inside his soul. Riot acts are being handed out. If people got caught in the store with merchandise, their charges got dropped. They had to have been caught outside of the store with merchandise to really get in trouble. Everything else they were dropping charges on and letting people out.

850 Bryant is right by the freeway. "Zzrrrom, zzroom," is all Jack could hear though he had no idea what the sound was. He kept reminding himself he was going to be all right, and after who knows how many days he hears, "Robertson, Robertson."

Jack stands up, "I'm right here."

"Roll it up, I've been calling you. If I had to one more time, I was maybe going to let you stay the night again. Charges dropped." Shuffling outside, Jack wondered how many days he was there. Two? Three? Four? Probably.

Outside Jack can barely hear what anyone is saying. Everything is underwater while he hoofs it up to the Haight. Strolling his direction, Ariel stops, and Jack tells him what happened. "Well, I'm gonna babysit you, Jack. Have you eaten?" he says with purpose.

"No, I'm starving." Jack confesses.

Ariel is a hustler. A Deadhead, he did west coast tours, and they'd rage Berkeley, Isla Vista, and even Laguna Beach together. That morning, in Oakland, if you sat through Sunday Service, they'd serve you fried chicken, sweet potato, black eyed peas, and collard greens. The guys ate large. Jack felt his skin again, like he climbed back into his actual shell, closing back in on the fabric of existence everyone else was in.

After lunch, they walked and shoplifted some oranges. Ariel said, "Hey, there's this girl that has the hots for me. We'll go see if maybe we can stay the night over there, and she's got a roommate too, some punk rocker girl." He wanted to hook him up, while Jack was barely at baseline, orbiting around humanity. Semi-functioning, he was coming out of the haze.

The small apartment was cool, and a settling vibe took over Jack. Ariel went into the bedroom with the Vanessa, and Jack was making sense out of words again and talking with her friend, Katie.

"Were you like interested?" he asked her.

"No, not even. His teeth were so awful, I remember he said it was genetic, like he and his mom had bad teeth. Hell no, he smoked meth or something. His teeth were so disgusting!" They laughed together at the misfortune.

He responds, "I guess it's hard to get a good dentist over there."

"Yeah," she says. "So do you skate?"

"Yeah, all the time. Coulda been pro for sure," he laughs.

"Yeah, me too."

"You do?"

"Yeah,"

"Oh, that's hot. What kind of board you got?"

"Rippin' Powell Cab, with a Chinese dragon. My brother gave it to me."

"Where do you skate? And do you skate in that mini skirt you're wearing?"

"You're fucking silly. Want to smoke some weed?"

"Do I want to smoke some weed? Yes, please. With you, yes." It's possible to have fun again, Jack is comfortable. She loads a nice glass hammer, and they smoke. Jack pulls the pipe from his mouth, and the herb completely hooked the psychedelic back. "And then they tried underneath the house grape watermelon limp dick with mint?" Katie stared at him while his words were stolen from his very tongue. But the last straw, "somewhere inside of that cunt's womb, there was an airplane and we went into a big ass bondage swing to Kentucky buck naked and it flew so high, over and under, over and under" prompts her to knock on her roommate's bedroom door.

"What?" an interrupted voice from inside chimed.

"Dude's gone whacky on me, he's creeping me out," she says.

The roommate cracks the door and looks at Jack. "I'm inside the robe plane plant spaceship, it's from there and here plus they said we're going to eat each other out on a bus," he says with a glary enthusiasm. Katie shakes her head.

Outside, Ariel and Jack walk across the street, away from her apartment and make their way to the park. Concerned, Ariel asked her for a blanket, and she gave in after a solid three second hesitation. They crash on the grass and pull the blanket over themselves. Freezing, they spoon, wake up and Ariel says calmly, "There's three crackheads standing over us." There are two guys fighting and pulling back and forth on the pipe, wrestling over the next hit.

Slowly, Ariel gets up and crawls away with the blanket. Spacey Jack is nonplussed until he hears, "Jack, come on motherfucker. Get up." He crawls up the grass and they wandered off to somewhere completely different.

I Need You to Shove This Up Your Cooch

Tour landed in Vermont that summer in 1994. This was only the third time the band played this northeastern state, the first was in 1978, and the second in 1983. It was a sunny July day at Franklin County Field, a huge swath of land that outfitted local fairs and airplane landings. The massive traffic jam getting there, and the heat made it unforgettable.

Lots of old school busses were on that tour. Heather and Max arrived in the lot at Highgate with their three-year-old daughter, Cassady, in their '47 International. Lance and Regina parked their Blue Bird in front of them. Josh and Melinda parked their '58 Chevy Apache next to them.

After the show, the lot was bubbling. Heather sold cheap hemp clothing and cool psychedelic 3D hat pins. When it was time to leave, the kids on the school busses decided to caravan out together. Strength in numbers. Their plan was to pull off the highway at the first stop with somewhere to eat.

The school busses drove off the grassy parking lot and onto the 78. They made it about four miles until bright flashing lights inhabited their entire space. Vermont State Troopers revved up their green Chevy Caprices and surrounded them, forcing them to pull over to the side, for no reason. All four busses maneuvered as safely as possible while the lot not too far behind was emptying out astronomical amounts of cars to the highway. The pigs corralled them like an oil man's herd of cattle and drew their guns.

Inside the International, Max sat at the steering wheel, nervous but calm. Heather held Cassady tight in her lap. She was just drifting to sleep, but the commotion startled her awake. Also aboard were Violet and Peter, two good friends who needed a ride out of Vermont. They were going to meet up with some other kids in New York before heading to RFK. Peter was frantic. The cops mobilized outside and prepared their arms to board the busses.

"Fuck," the word escaped Heather's lips as everyone was thinking it. The troopers knocked on the door and Max opened it up for them slowly. The first asshole came up the steps with his pistol drawn.

"Everyone on your feet. Now. Line up against that side. Let's go." Not one indication of why they were pulled over escaped his mouth. The kids moved, Heather holding Cassady tight and a little higher up so she could set her head up on her shoulder. The little one wasn't too phased, just going with the flow. It had been a long day frolicking on the airfield lawn, having fun with the other children, chasing bubbles, eating fruit rollups, picking at the grass, and dancing everywhere the music played. She was clearly trying to get a nap in.

The trooper surveyed, there was a small couch against the wall, so it was tight with everyone on their feet in the middle. "Okay, everyone, sit down on the couch. Go on."

Max gently lowered himself down, he was tired. He didn't get much sleep the last few days, it was a long drive out from the west coast. Finally hitting their groove, finding their friends on the lot, and being together revived him but he was starving and ready to eat. Violet was scared, she had some doses but shoved them inside her bra as soon as the lights appeared and was still considering eating them. Peter scooted up next to Heather on the far end and whispered in her ear while two other assholes boarded the bus with their guns.

"I just got out of jail. I cannot go back to jail," he said to her with puppy dog eyes. "I need you to shove this up your cooch." She looked slyly over to him, not moving her face, and sees a small brick of hash in his hand.

"What?" she questioned him quietly. He said nothing, the assholes were starting to look them up and down, guns drawn, one at a time, Max, Violet, Peter and finally in Heather's direction. They were like parasites searching for a way to take them down. First stop their bus, then make them sit, then find their drugs. The DEA was right outside, in plain clothes, waiting to see what the troopers could deliver. Taxpayers' money funded Operation Dead Ahead, just another chapter in the war on the drugs.

Heather held Cassady close to her chest but considered Peter's words for a hot second. She didn't want him to get in trouble. She imagined quickly how she'd take the brick and push it right up into her vagina, underneath her dress, in front of everyone on the bus. But she looked at Peter, at his scared face, and whispered, "I can't do that. I have a child. I can't help you because of my daughter."

Peter was tweaking hard at this point, and just as the cop raised a gun in his direction, he shoved the brick inside the couch behind him. It had a small pull-out bed inside, and he felt into the tiny mattress section and shoved it in as far as his hand could reach.

The assholes studied them with their beady lifeless eyes and intimidation. "Is there anything illegal on this bus?" one barked. "You? You're the owner, you were driving. What's your name?"

Max was calm, the main thing on his mind was his daughter and Heather, but of course, he had no idea what Violet or Peter might have on them. No way would he ever throw anyone under the bus, so to speak. "I am the owner. Max Hartman. There is nothing illegal on this bus to my knowledge," he told them.

"To your knowledge? I hope you're real smart then," he retorted. They continued to heavily question them, asking the same things, 'who are you, where are you going, are you sure you don't have any drugs on this bus?' Guns drawn, the questioning was excessive, Cassady whimpered. Max was uneasy. Heather kept her hand on Cassady's head, so she didn't turn around and face the monsters. Finally exhausted of all the dead-end answers, the troopers wanted blood.

“Get up,” one said to Heather. “Now. Get up and hand your daughter to your friend and step off the bus.” She listened, stood up with Cassady and delicately handed her to Max. The cop escorted her off the bus and outside into the horrifying menagerie of a DEA investigation in full swing. The troopers had boarded each bus, flashlights and guns were everywhere. She watched Josh and Melinda get off the Apache, while a few more cops went onboard. They were discussing something inside the bus, but she couldn’t make out what the problem was. Melinda caught her eye and nodded her head but offered a small smile. She dosed earlier and was still able to connect with the higher space in this terrifying moment. Nothing left to do but smile, smile, smile.

Heather made eyes at the Apache, wondering what they were doing. Melinda shook her head just slightly enough to say, ‘don’t worry about it.’ In the next second, a gun fired inside the bus! They all looked over and the pigs inside were kicking at something metal, there were reverberations emulating out of the old school bus innards. The men stomped around and finally exited the bus frustrated. Josh kept a solemn face, he was angry, but what could he do? There are zero rights in these situations, none. This is the lawman’s greatest effort against the liberation of consciousness, even in 1994, some thirty plus years after psychedelics hit the city streets.

A DEA taskforce agent spoke up first, “Well?”

“Nothing. It’s empty,” a trooper responded. Josh kept a small safe on the bus, underneath his couch. When they found it, they were sure they hit gold. But Josh wouldn’t open it without a search warrant to which they laughed and pushed him and Melinda off the bus. The DEA ordered agents to shoot the lock on the safe and bust it open.

A goon brought Heather over to the back of one of the Caprice’s. A thick three-ring binder sat on the trunk, and he was poised for show and tell. “Open it,” he told her. She did what the bully said and inside were many plastic sleeves with polaroid photos fit into each cell. "Do you know that person?"

"Which one?" she said. There were four on each page.

"Do you know this person?" he pointed to the first photo, a young woman with reddish-brown hair and beautiful beaded earrings.

"No."

"How about this person?" he pointed to the next photo, an image with way too much light on the subject, an indigenous man about fifty years old with a ponytail.

"Nope."

"Well, keep looking," he turned to pages for her, "look at every person." Heather stared at each image and turned the pages. Faces and faces of Deadheads in the sleeves, this was their data arsenal. "Do you know anyone?"

"I don't. I mean, I don't really recognize anyone. I've maybe seen some of these faces before, but I don't know anyone. I don't know their names," she said. But she was thinking, 'holy fuck!' There were a lot of her friends in the book. He kept turning the pages for her, one after another, and she saw many people she knew well. At the end of the book, he looked at Heather hard, the gaze of a skeptical asshole.

"Get back on the bus."

She climbed back in, and two goons had ransacked the insides. She could see her clothes taken out of bags, drawers opened, and things tossed around haphazardly. Peter's eyes widened when he saw her. She sat back down next to him, and he gave her a small sly smile. They hadn't opened the couch.

No one was arrested. The couple hours with the spineless excuses for human beings left everyone so hungry they could barely speak. The busses rolled away, and with the same plan intact, they pulled off at the first Denny's.

The glass doors of the busy diner swung open for them by a

pair of undercovers going outside to have a smoke. Max and Josh couldn't even muster a laugh, and Peter shook his head. "They're everywhere." A waitress seated them and served them up glasses of water and a few coffees. Heather ordered a couple of hot chocolates for her and Cassady. Strange people dressed in khakis, Hawaiian shirts, and outdoor gear that made zero sense at 1 a.m. in this neighborhood reminded Max of John Carpenter's film, *They Live*. The zombies landed and they were all eating a Grand Slam.

Their waitress, Sally, did everything she could to give them a sweet experience, but that place was hot. Eyes were everywhere. Heather and Melinda could barely eat, the narcs made them feel sick to their stomachs. Peter finished his club sandwich and threw his dollars down. "I'm going to get a ride out with Stevie." There was another table of kids nearby leaving.

"You get everything?" Heather said.

"I did. Love you, kids."

Spinning

The cute guy at Minerva's high school bought her a ticket to her first show. She was a senior, seventeen years old and wanted to check out the music.

"Jerry's not looking so great," he explained as they found their seats in the side section of the large indoor stadium. Minerva had no idea what he meant by that but ingested the information with compassion. She didn't know what to say back, or if she needed to say anything. She didn't. What was most intriguing her at that moment was the fashion, the styles everyone wore, the fabrics, the patterns, and the way people inhabited their digs. They were happy and it felt creative. There was a momentum building.

Minerva enjoyed her first show with the cute guy. She experienced an extraordinary time dancing with him and the thousands of other Deadheads who took up as much space as they could wherever they found their place. She banged her knees against the seat in front of her all night while she boogied. The next day, they were all bruised.

At Minerva's next show, she wandered around to find a better place to dance. Taking the stairwell, she gave that a shot but quickly realized it was not safe, she could easily fall. Walking through the area between the concert hall and the hallways, she discovered the small space cordoned off by drapes that the kids usually opened during the show. There was a slight slant, but she danced there for an entire set. It wasn't totally working for her.

During the next set, she danced there but pushed down to the end of the area. Almost in the hallway but not quite, she found a groove and so much energy, she started jumping up and down. So connected and yet boundless, she could feel herself leaping into the music, she was jumping and jumping and jumping and started spinning, spinning, spinning.

For the next run of shows, Minerva knew where to go and really found herself spinning to the sound, like a pinwheel in the wind. Her head would cock to the side, and she would take note of her posture and try to keep straight because she could feel a white light come down and move through her body. Moving in and out and around, she could also receive the energy and be in a peaceful space where she didn't even feel like she was moving. It was still and almost quiet, pure grace.

This evolved out into the hallways, and into a gift, a prayerful space to be one with the universe, with everyone and everything. She learned to spin high and low, bringing the energy up and out, moving it around and sharing it with the other dancers around her. There were so many styles of dancing everywhere and the crew brought speakers out into the hallways to enhance the sonic layers of performance. People would kind of roll onto each other, with heavy body contact that sometimes looked like a wave. There were people snapping their fingers and tapping their feet in an almost vaudeville showtune number. Some couples would dance straight out of the fifties, throwing themselves around and commanding an audience from the stadium vendors. Minerva made fantastic friends on the dancefloor.

She wore a long psychedelic patterned skirt. Alternating with her friends, the girls would sneak in mushroom tea in a jar between their legs. Sometimes they would dance behind the stage in the hallway. The wider the hallway the better. At set break, Minerva went to the Phil Zone, an area in the seats above stage left, to get stoned. The kids used to pass around beautiful glass pipes and after their hit, they'd raise the pipe to their foreheads giving thanks to the herb and the moment they were in together. Weed was so illegal, they'd hold onto their hit for dear life, knowing they may not get another one.

Three months later, Jerry fell into a coma.

BMWNO2

Five pounds of weed is 20k easy on the east coast. Bernie and Kurt knew it was worth the wait and drank their coffees and smoked cigarettes in Glenn's living room. Glenn is Bernie's oldest brother, he moved to Philadelphia when Bernie was fourteen years old and has been able to run herb through a few different channels bringing in cash without much effort.

"You want to watch a movie?" Glenn asks.

"Sure, whatcha got?" Bernie asks.

"Got any porn?" Kurt chides.

"Oh, yeah, there's a gay porn mart on Main Street."

"I knew you would know where."

"Fuck, I have some movie channels." He flips through the cable selections with the remote. Kurt's pager vibrates in his pocket. He checks the device, it's Sickboy: "Yo, RFK, get out here."

"Sickboy," Kurt explains.

"What's he want?" Bernie chimes in.

"He wants us to head out to RFK."

"Yeah, well, shit."

"We're just sitting here."

"Yeah, sure. Mine as well," Bernie sighs. "I'm game."

"What?" Glenn asks. "You're going to the show?"

"Fuck it," Kurt adds.

"Page me if anything happens, otherwise I'll see you in the morning."

Later that night, after the show, Bernie and Kurt rage a party at the Marriott with a tank. Abruptly, they take off with Sickboy and

Suzanne, some kids they know from Rochester. They climb in her nice black BMW and head to another hotel for more privacy, meaning cocaine and space to spread out. Sickboy took the tank with him and laid it down on the center console of the car. A section of like four feet of garden hose is duck taped to the top so nobody hits right off the tank, and it's doesn't freeze their mouth.

Seemingly coherent and arguably the best person to drive, Suzanne focuses on the road. Sickboy navigates the stereo next to her in the passenger seat and hits the tank. Bernie hits it after and then Kurt hits it long. Somewhere inside the auditory twilight zone of hallucination and comfort, he tosses the hose back up to the front. With a good handle on the transit adventure, Suzanne hits the tank while she's driving.

Watching for cops is the number one priority when driving a car late at night on the east coast. Sometimes though, you wait for the safe space, the settled in feeling that you have a stake on this highway, you and your automobile have a say, even set a vibe for the flow. Perhaps that's when you pop open a cold one, or light up that joint, or take back a couple pills. But when is the right time to hit the nitrous tank? Who's to say?

Her tight grip on the steering wheel crumbled in a nanosecond after her hit.

"She's fishing out dude!" Bernie stammered.

Her body folds in on itself like origami. The car drifts quickly to the side of the highway, hitting the street reflectors and graded asphalt meant to slow cars down. "Fuck! We're gonna crash!" Kurt screams.

Sickboy grabs the wheel and veers the car, he straightens it out. Suzanne slumps into the fabric of her chair.

"Hey!" Sickboy screams at her. "Hey!" He slaps her face hard. She wakes up. He pulls the car to the side, and she steps on the brakes slowly.

Kurt reaches up and takes the hose to his mouth. The tank is done. "It was good while it lasted," he admits.

Tragedy Nearly Diverted

Two separate New Jersey State Troopers drove steadily on Highway 95. In front of them, a car loomed. The beat-up sedan wavered in the lane, a little too slow, a little too fast at times.

Joey was asleep in the backseat of Francisco's car, they were on JGB fall tour. The passenger side right windows were busted out and the frame was all bent in between the windows because of the accident in Boulder. But they made it to Jersey, dready, Guatemalan, and all raggedy.

Lights went on in their background. The reds flashed on and off, on and off, and Francisco looked in the mirror. "Shit." The two state troopers were pulling him over.

He pulled to the right and hugged the curb. The troopers exited their vehicles, eager. Joey was still sleeping soundly in the backseat until he heard a tap on the window, that loud police baton TAP. The worst sound to hear from a cop aside from a gun firing.

"We need the bags of weed," the cop orders. Joey wakes up and starts stuffing bags of weed into the seats, out of sight. Francisco throws his wallet back to him as nonchalantly as possible. They were four sheets sticking out of it. They were bigger than the wallet, which fell right onto the floor. Joey couldn't reach for it; it was in plain view on the floor with the sheet sticking out. Copper number two peers in at Joey and questions his existence.

"So, what do you have? In the car?"

Francisco was wearing a big fat rainbow fanny pack.

"Let me see that please." He points to his waistline and expects it immediately, but Francisco takes a minute to remove it and hand it over. The first cop feels it up, opens it and notices a Ziploc with white crystalline powder along the bottom. "What's this?" he asks, holding it out.

"It's crushed Sudafed. I'm coughing a lot and if I eat too much or too little it makes me sleepy or speedy. It's crushed Sudafed, that's all."

The other cop studies the bag. "It doesn't look like cocaine."

It was ecstasy, like a quarter ounce of ecstasy. The cop gave it back. But he took the weed inside, and Francisco appealed, "I don't care about the Sudafed. You think you could give us the weed back? Because, you know, we sit in a circle in the woods and it's our meditation."

The cops looked at each other, in the eyes. They thought about it and knew right away that right thing to do was give it back. They looked in the trunk but didn't bother to search any of the backpacks. They moved things around and then moved on. They handed the weed back to Francisco.

"Alright then, get out of here." The tin men began to walk away but Joey stopped them and handed one a smoky quartz crystal.

"Thanks," he said with blank eyes.

Francisco drove away with all the bags of pot, and the sheets and the fucking ecstasy and everything. "Put this on your mantle at home," Joey had said as he handed the large crystal over, "take it to your wife."

Shit Bus

A low hum hovered through the lot. Some kids were locked out, but most made it in that night. A couple hours passed and suddenly, the sound of doors opening around the Coliseum traveled through the cold night air.

Everyone poured out of the show. Cigarettes light up left and right, as if the spark came from the electric vibe in the air. People are smiling, euphoric, saved from another night in the totally absurd fabric of existence.

Henry and Kimberly walked out of the show towards their friend Gary who was being swallowed by the lot as they stared out at the sea of heads. Miracled in the show right before it started, they left their big Labrador Smoky in the bus with a window cracked.

When they got back and opened the door, Smoky jumped out and was covered in shit. The inside of the bus was wallpapered entirely in shit! It looked like he pointed his ass and it exploded! Shit was on the ceilings, the walls, and all their belongings. Smoky ran all over that bus with an exploding ass.

'That is the most disgusting thing I've ever seen,' Gary thought.

Henry and Kimberly stood around outside. He looked to her and finally said, "What the fuck do we even do?"

The Procurer of Rare Music

One particular venue on tour in northern California had quite the slant. General admission lawn seating was a lot of fun but could be merciless on your body dancing through a show. The only reprieve was along the very top where the grass hill flattened out, this was a prime dance location. A magical amphitheater, nonetheless, it was a time before Google and the other big money tech pundits moved into the neighborhood and carved up the stolen land with their industrial office buildings.

Evelyn was eight months pregnant and sitting on this very lawn, circled up with her friends, puffing fatties before the show. Their kind bud burned nicely and drifted through the air of pre-show excitement.

Backstage, a trio of roadies took flight on a mission. Coming up the side of the lawn, they wandered through the audience searching. Lingering in their direction, the choice herb caught on and peaked their interest. They slowly approached Evelyn's circle.

"We like the weed you're smoking," the tall one complimented.

"We don't have any weed backstage, could we trade you a backstage pass for some of your weed?" asked the other roadie with dirty blonde hair.

The kids were honored and more than willing to part with a handful of nice-sized buds for the crew. This is how Evelyn ended up backstage at Shoreline.

She came into the backside pavilion just past the stage and encountered a huge spread of food. A little nervous, she didn't know anyone but at eight months pregnant was flashed smile after smile. A bunch of limos were lined up nearby and a group of small children were having the time of their lives playing with a bunch of kittens. A nanny hovered over them, catching the loose kittens as they attempted their wild escapes. 'What a killer job,' Evelyn thought.

A fly on the wall, she didn't say anything to anyone for awhile. She ate some food and sat to the side by herself. Until a man with a long walrus-type mustache with graying hair and a nice leather hat walked through the area. She knew him. He carried a briefcase and was out on the lot with the kids all the time. She knew his name and would always say hello. Every time she saw him, she wondered what was in his briefcase. He saw her and walked over.

"Whoa, Evelyn, you're backstage?"

"Yeah, we traded weed for a pass. But it's kinda boring," she admitted to him. "I don't know anybody."

"What do you think of Edie Brickell?" he asked.

"She's alright, I know everybody's into her," she told him. Evelyn wasn't that into it her, but Edie and her whole scene were backstage hanging out and he was making friendly conversation.

"Well, look, Evelyn, when the show is over, just come stand with me. Okay?" She eyed him over. "Trust me," he affirmed, "I want you to stand with me."

"Okay," she said.

A couple hours and some change later, the show ends with a killer *Mighty Quinn*. Evelyn finds her friend and stands next to him. He's clutching his briefcase and Phil walks offstage and directly to him. They start talking about music obsessively and Evelyn watches as her friend opens his briefcase and takes out some records. 'Wow,' she thought, 'he's really friendly with Phil.' Their enthusiasm for music was precious, and he gave Phil the records he was hyping.

"Thank you," Phil told him, with childlike excitement, like the kids with the kittens. On and on they talked about this band and that album, that year, that sound, and Evelyn thought, 'Okay, this is boring.' She turned away readying her own escape and ran smack dab into Jerry! Her huge pregnant belly on her eighteen-year-old body! Jerry laughed and laughed, and she did too, not sure how else to react. She smiled at him and thought, 'oh my god, I'm getting the fuck out of here, I don't even know what to say to these guys.'

In her friend's ear, she slipped in, "I'm going to find my people." He smiled at her and gave the 'it's cool' nod.

Evelyn reunited with her scene and got comfortable again. Later she wandered through the front part of the lot by all the trees and saw her friend.

"What was all that about?" she asked him finally.

"I procure rare music for the Grateful Dead," he answered.

Jack in the Lot

On one of the five night runs that winter in Oakland she met him dancing in the hallway. They puffed, shared water, and lamented over the loss of the New Year's show. After the encore, they were a ball of happy sweat with long curly dark hair.

Outside they wandered the lot together, not wanting to leave each other's company. Theo was on his way out to Hawaii after these shows, and Linda was set to drive up to Mendocino, so every moment together was gold. He busted out his kind bud and rolled a nice fatty for them to share. Between a couple cars, they squeezed closer and closer, passing the joint and holding each other's eyes as long as they could. Terrence and Jolene stopped by for a second, hilarious elders engaged in their own playful frolic. They took a hit and moved on, super schwilly and looking for the short bus with the enchiladas.

Linda and Theo started holding hands. He told her about his tattoos, and she showed him where she wanted one. She gave him a look at some nugs she had, and he was impressed. She wasn't swingin' them, but she gave him a nugget just to see the sparkle in his eyes. Smelling deep into the flower, he noticed a man with a mustache and beard walking past. The man took notice of the adorable couple.

"Hello," he said in a curious friendly voice.

"Hi," she said.

"Do you kids want to smoke?" he asked, which was funny because Theo's nose was still deep in the crystals.

"Yeah, man, for sure," she told him. They moved out from

their small space into the wider aisle, and she nonchalantly looked him up and down. He was kind of short, carrying a satchel strung across his front. Jovial, he had the warmest face, and she could sense how genuine he was in his every move.

Theo gave him a hug. "What's up, man?"

"Hey, man, you guys have a good show?" He was searching his bag for his weed and a pipe.

"Yes, so much fun," Linda said. "What a good time!"

"It sure was," he said, and pulled out some books from his bag, still looking for his pipe. Once he found it, he loaded his herb inside and handed it to her. She took the green hit, a nice toke, and reveled in the taste immediately.

"Ooh, that's kind," she said and handed it to Theo. He puffed hard and let out a huge cloud.

"It is, isn't it," he smiled and took the pipe. While he was inhaling, Linda couldn't help but ask about his books. "Oh, these," he replied slyly as if he was going to show them a secret, but then shifted the energy to a humble sense of pride and handed her a copy of his book, *The Emperor Wears No Clothes.*

"Oh, I know about this," she told him, "I've looked through it before, wait, this is yours?"

He smiled again. "Yep, I'm Jack."

"Jack, I'm Linda, and this is Theo," she smiled and hit the pipe again hard.

"Man, that's some nice smoke," Theo told him.

"Hey, I'd like to buy a book." Rifling through her waist pouch she pulled out some cash. "How about ten dollars and a nug?" she asked, showing him her bounty.

"Deal."

Gerard

All the kids packed inside a room at the motel by the Coliseum. Monica washed her face in the small bathroom sink, scrubbing off the dirt and sweat from the long day. Micah cleaned his feet in the bathtub, they were disgustingly black from dancing. The show glow was all over their faces and conversations chatted up endlessly.

"Did you see him smile when they went into *Slip*?"

"That one dude would not shut up!"

"I saw her in the Phil Zone but lost her for the rest of the show!"

"It hit so hard, so quick, really not much of a grace period on that there dose."

"All I ate was that gooball and those french fries."

"Ohhh, that *Stella*!"

Smoke started to waft into the small bathroom, and like an alarm sounding, Monica and Micah finished up and joined the bedroom scene. Two double beds squeaked and squeaked as Justine, Chuck, and Pablo bounced around in joy, bumping each other over and over. The thin orange, yellow, pink polyester floral bedspread only slightly covered the shifty mattress. Mitchell passed a fatty from the other bed, while Kerry finished rolling another on the make-shift surface that acted like a desk and handed it to Ryan to light. Liz sealed hers and gave it to Isabelle to start up.

The fatties drifted through their hands, passed from one sister to another brother. Huge exhales filled the space and the insides of the conversation. The herb was more than fulfilling, it was a reward, a connection, the leash that led them into the circle of life.

Gerard sat next to Roberto on the bed, like a good boy, getting his fur pet behind the ears. This cute little pup had grown into a full-fledged highly credentialed tour dog. All the kids knew him, and he took rides at will.

There were almost as many dogs as kids in the room. Howl and Stella cuddled next to each other on the floor, happy to be inside and warm. At the other end, Nirvana, Gem, and Porter played with each other, and occasionally, Mitchell would stir 'em up more, until the fatty came back around and he'd stop to take a hit. Only Justice and Ray took the luxury of the room seriously, they jumped up on the bed and curled up onto the pillows as soon as they got inside. Snoring like the two cutest little mutts you ever saw, they jolted at the loud knock on the door.

Waiting maybe a half a second, the knock came again and again, ugly and persistent. The fatties went out, and Ryan popped a look through the crevice of the awfully thin window curtain and saw the cops. "Yep, six up," he whispered.

"Damnit," Kerry said. Everyone in the room made necessary adjustments and the knocks came again and again.

"Okay, ready?" Mitchell asked. Roberto almost laughed but nodded. Mitchell opened the door and three cops tried to come in but were halted by the dogs and the kids. They couldn't fit into the room, but they sure squeezed their way inside as much real estate as they could.

"Looks like you're exceeding the occupancy in here, guys," one pig stammered, holding the door wide open. On cue, all the dogs went wild, and ran past them, through their legs and right out the door.

Another one opened his mouth, "I'm pretty sure there's no dogs allowed in these rooms."

"Oh man, you let the dogs get out," Ryan whined like a true thespian. He put his backpack on and ran outside after the dogs.

"Hey, hey," the cop said to him, but saw it was useless, the dogs were running around outside in the parking lot like a wild pack and Ryan was trying to get Justice on a leash. All the kids stood up, ready to vacate. Roberto put his backpack on, trying to keep an eye on Gerard, who was way out there, already looking for ground score in the bushes. Kerry, Monica, Micah walked out, and Roberto followed. As he passed the threshold, hoping these cops were not going any further than kicking them out, Gerard ran all the way back to the door and bit the cop in the leg!

"Ahhhh! I'm going to shoot that dog!" the cop squealed. Gerard scurried back out to Roberto and followed the kids as they looked for somewhere else to stay.

The War on Drugs

Only an hour before showtime, the lot was pulsing, and Belinda pulled off her tee shirt. She had a tie dye bikini top on underneath. The sun was sweltering, and her acid was kicking in. Waiting patiently for her boyfriend Victor, she was holding it down, leaning on a parked car, excited for the show. She'd only seen the band a few times before, and only close to where she lived because she didn't drive yet. But in five days, Belinda would celebrate her sweet sixteen, and she was looking forward to getting her driver's license as much as she was to the trip the dose was beginning to take her on.

Victor let out a subtle, "Hey!" to get her attention. His acid was settling in too and he had a little more business to do before going inside. Belinda made her way to him, a few aisles over. She figured he scored, since the messaging was on the downlow, and she could see he was looking around to make sure they were safe. He took her hand and led her down the aisle a few cars further to an old, faded orange Dodge van with Idaho plates.

They both took another solid look around before Victor rapped on the side door. It creaked open and a friendly face smiled and waved them inside. The temperature in the van was at least ten degrees more than outside and sweat dripped down Belinda's stomach as she sat cross-legged across from a couple who had weight in boomers. So much so there were a few garbage bags tied off. One was open and a woman with long blond dreadlocks and a beautiful handmade dress took out handfuls of cubensis and weighed out an ounce. She handed it to Belinda. "How much?" she asked her politely.

"A hundred and twenty is fine." It was a killer deal for these parts at this time and Belinda didn't hesitate to produce the cash. She took the ounce and put it inside her small Guate tote bag with the rest of her belongings. Before going in the show, she'd put the ounce down her pants to hide it from security, but it was far too hot to do it right then.

"One more?" she asked Victor.

"Yep." He took out his money and counted it while she carefully weighed all the caps and stems on a small digital scale. She smiled and gave him his bag. "Thanks so much."

The deal was smooth. When they stepped out of the van, the sun was relentless, like an old flame forcing to rekindle a connection. Belinda pulled her hair back in her scrunchie, trying to get it higher off her neck. Victor took out some water and guzzled it, he was parched. Just as the sky was yellow and the sun was blue, they took a few steps away and started to head into the show.

Walking leisurely, Belinda noticed a few oversized steroid-looking men start to circle up. They were a little ways from them, but she spotted their khaki shorts and trademark Hawaiian shirts and knew something was wrong. She watched them surround the area. They moved in like rabid hyaenas who hadn't had a meal in days. It was too late. A big man three times her size grabbed her arm and forced her to the side. Another man grabbed Victor and shoved him up against a car. Two more narcs moved in on another young man who was standing nearby smoking a cigarette.

The creaky sound of the orange van door opening was followed by a, "Get up and out of the vehicle right now. Drop everything and do it now or we'll take you out ourselves."

A few other kids were dropped to the ground harshly by some undercovers, and with their faces in the light brown dirt the pigs took their backpacks and rifled through. No questions, no queries, not even a 'what's your name?' Law enforcement took the couple inside the van out, slammed them up against the wall and cuffed them. Three DEA agents dressed as fake tourists went through their van, dumping out their personal belongings everywhere and stole the garbage bags full of mushrooms.

The large roided human who looked like he was on his family vacation at Disneyland opened Belinda's bag without asking. He threw out her pack of cigarettes, her lip balm, and finally forked out her ounce of mushrooms and another small bag of weed. It was all her head stash.

No Miranda Rights read anywhere on this scene, and at least eight people in custody so far. They made a perimeter and arrested every person in it, less than an hour before showtime at the outdoor venue in this small part of hell.

At the end of the eighties, the lot had been so ransacked by undercovers, in every big city they were easy to spot. The tourist was the dominant costume of the clandestine role-playing cop targeting humans who have or sell drugs. This Monopoly outtake was the main character of the dehumanizing psychology of law enforcement. Turn on the stranger to town, the harmless visitor, the jaded traveler! Could it be they channeled a pretty standard understanding of most drug dealers, that anyone who is following all the rules of capitalism, the nine to five with benefits, pension, and vacation, dressed in privileged holidaying attire advertised in outdoor magazines, really needed to get high. It's the unwoke, the straight and entitled looking for adventure, release, and a brush with real mental freedom. The perfect custy should look like they need drugs badly and have plenty of money to pay for them, hence the tourist narc was born. Was it an inspired character from Masonic theater rituals? Will anyone ever know?

The kids on the lot called out the cops when they could, rapidly disseminating the information to everyone who needed to know and if the thugs did slip into circles unseen, it wasn't long before someone was popped so everyone knew who was really who.

Belinda did not have a record. She was a minor and never even had a traffic ticket. A straight A student, out with her boyfriend Victor, who was only a year older and the most promising science student at their high school, the show was an early birthday present to her. Victor bought their tickets and arranged for them to get a ride with an older friend who had a car. Where was George? They left him drinking beer on Shakedown when they set out on the mission. They had all dropped together, so that when they got back to each other they'd be perfectly pickled to go into the show.

A white van pulled up and everyone arrested were bound to each other in chains and loaded in one at a time up to the used torn vinyl bench seats. Belinda was so high; all she could do was smile and Victor looked at her and shook his head. "We're gonna miss the show," he whispered to her as though that was the worst of their problems. In that exact moment, that was the only thing on his mind.

"Shut up!" the loud, roid cop shouted. "I don't want to hear one peep out of any of you." Belinda held in her laughter. What was this large white rooster with muscles bigger than his head squawking about? She took a breath and did everything she could to not laugh. He looked slimy to her, the sweat finally showing itself on the cops' angry brows. Belinda and Victor could see evil dripping out of his pores, and she wanted to laugh at him so hard she had to take a few more breaths to make the funny dissipate.

A scratchy but effective Chevy engine powered the van. They winded out of the parking lot to a side delivery lane that went right under the concert venue. Where were they being taken? To a security substation made up of a few large rooms, one of which was the command center with a small pen for holding prisoners.

Belinda realized these thugs were the county Sheriffs. They unattached her and Victor from the rest of the line because they were minors and sat them down at a large table in front of the holding cell. The gravity of this new location enveloped them. Reaching a peak, the acid was terrific. Victor and George scooped up the gels on Shakedown and the timing was perfect. The walls were breathing, and they could hear the opener playing above, *Come on and let the good times roll.*

"What's your name?" A woman with many coats of beige make-up and muscles so big she was as deformed as her male counterparts obstructed Belinda's eyeline. "What's your name?"

Belinda was not sure if she wanted to tell them.

"There was no ID card in your bag. I went through it."

The woman was a monster! Her eyes were distorted and uneven, her skin was crawling up and down her skull as though it was looking for a way out. There was an animal inside trapped, and her uniform and atrocious body language was holding it down. Belinda had to face the mutant.

"Belinda."

"Oh, that's good. Last name?"

"Williamson."

"Date of birth?"

"June ninth."

"Year?"

"1989."

"Not this year."

Belinda just stared at her, she's answering the beast's questions, what more could she need besides a facial and a frontal lobotomy?

"What year were you born?"

Polka dots swarmed the room. It was a party. Belinda could hear, "Now the race is on, and here comes pride in the backstretch." The show must go on. Humming along to the band, Belinda was having fun. The Sheriff did not like this. She grew more hostile, dulling her aura into stagnancy, and her ears turned into long demented gorgons with fumes billowing out of their eyes.

"Is this your bag?"

"You took it from me."

"I didn't."

"Your man did." Belinda began to really watch the room. There was a lot of activity, blinking lights, radio conversations, and occasionally a frozen moment where all the officers' brains seemed to stop working, as if they were all being recalibrated, and then naturally continued what they were doing. Their tiny minds could only take small amounts of uploading at a time. In between, they stomped around the substation in their obtuse bodybuilder frames.

"How did you get to the show?"

"In a car."

"Funny."

Belinda tried to bring her attention back to this wretched woman, but the sideshow was entertaining.

"Who drove the car?"

"A friend."

"Him?" She pointed to Victor who was studying the same sideshow Belinda was enjoying.

"Nope," she said. Belinda was not a rat; she knew to tell them as little as possible and use the word 'lawyer' if needed.

But that satisfied the monster. As she got up to leave, Belinda felt her predatory eyes scan her body and take in her bikini top. She looked at the woman, who condemned her summertime outfit jealously. Overall, she was angry that these druggy hippie freak heathens existed. This woman trained hard to work at this level with men, and she had partnered up with the DEA before. This wasn't her first rodeo. It was a Sheriff operation, but during the war on drugs, the DEA always had their crew in the shadows, and when it was their time to take over, it was just as clunky as the design of handcuffs. Trapped to her role, the woman could do everything the men could and better but had to hold even her vile self back and stay in her place.

At the head table of this banquet of imbeciles, a Sheriff sat writing a report. He looked up at Belinda's bikini top, and like the other monster, his mouth drooled over her cleavage and tanned skin. Another roided out ape Sheriff fi fi fo fummed his way to the table and stared directly at Belinda's bikini top the entire distance. This was enough for her. They were leeches, unbridled carnivores with zero bedside manner.

"Can I please get my tee shirt? From my bag that you took?" The cops froze, they were stunned she spoke up the way she did. No one said a word to her. The woman came back towards them and sat with the men. A strange reptile show began, they spoke to each other with long and pointed tongues and grew inflated humps in their shoulders. These oafs knew nothing of intellect, they were purely reactionary and took too long trying to compute what they should do, if they could be predatory or ethical.

"Can I please have my tee shirt?" They all looked up at her again, how dare she speak. Victor smiled but suppressed the disgust he had at all these low-level humans. Anytime they looked in Belinda's direction, he took a couple deep breaths and reminded himself they would eventually leave. He knew they weren't going into a cell; he'd had friends who went to Juvy. After selling weed and acid in their suburb over the last year, he had a small handle on their consequences—and how being sixteen years old was a benefit.

Finally, the lizard woman stood up. She placated the men by bending over to read something specific on the report, and they drooled over her ruptured flesh pushed into her polyster county circus uniform. Every bulge was something they could hunt with their flat eyes. "Ha, ha, ha, ha!" they all laughed at a typo. "I bet Gonzalez wrote this, English is his second language, you know," the woman cackled.

"Hello?" Belinda echoed. Each second that passed, the bullies around the room stared at her bikini top, and she was not there to be an objectified model prisoner.

The gang looked over, shocked again at this bold use of communication. The woman steamed like a kettle, but this was her lane and she decided to navigate it before there was an order from a dominant male creature. Slowly she obliged and the men watched her shuffle through the large clear bags of evidence. Her body bent over the table and all the subhuman male gazes in the room plastered on to her ass. This was not lost on Victor and Belinda, who were exchanging knowing looks at each other, trying desperately not to laugh out loud.

Patrick, the guy nabbed in the lot who was smoking a cigarette when the sting went down, was in the holding cell right behind them. In his late twenties, he had a quarter of weed in his pocket and was just getting his head together in the hot sun and taking a reprieve from being on Shakedown. A Sheriff goon came from behind him, grabbed his shoulders and shook him down immediately. Pretty high too, a brother he ran into on the lot gave him some killer liquid and he had just scored a ticket. This moment in the substation was not lost on him either. "They might actually eat her," he whispered to the sequestered minors.

"Yuck, can't imagine that would be nourishing at all," Victor whispered back. Belinda was doing everything in her power to not laugh—her permasmile so wide, she had to look like the Joker. The thugs were so focused on the woman they weren't aware there was a sidebar.

"Between them all, there must be 3 gallons of spray tan," he said back.

"I don't think they breathe the same way we do," Victor observed. In a loving tone, he quickly added, "are you going to be okay? You have anyone to help you?"

The guy nodded subtly. "Family will bail me out, hopefully I make tomorrow's show."

Victor nodded back sadly. He knew there was a wrath coming from his conservative parents. Not in any hurry, he contemplated minimally about their reaction, but still concerned on a far deeper level about missing the shows. Upstairs he could hear, "*Tell me the cost; I can pay, let me go, tell me love is not lost. Sell everything; without love day to day insanity's king.*"

Belinda's bag was the last one the goon found. She opened it, took the tee shirt out and a small plastic phone book. As if it was a delicate gesture, she offered her the tee placing it on the table. Belinda's posture perked up.

"You gonna put it on for me?" The woman loathed her for asking.

"No. I'm not." She squared her own posture for a beat. An obligatory gesture to remind Belinda who was in control. Belinda waited patiently; she could hear *Help on the Way* too. The idiot came around behind her and slowly undid her handcuffs. Free of the restraints, Belinda rolled her wrists out a few times to release the stress and slipped on her shirt. Relieved, Victor sat up a little straighter to stretch his torso out.

The woman returned to the command desk and showed one of the men Belinda's address book. They were all looking through a giant three-ring binder of Polaroids in plastic sleeves, paging through color images of human beings marked and tagged for associating with illegal drug use. One of the men flipped through Belinda's address book, looking for subversive elements that could help their case against her. Under his breath he said something to the woman. Belinda heard a slithering sound, like a snake. The Sheriff squad became snake-like, with red eyes and weird scaly spray tanned skin. A narrative continued in Belinda's expansive mind, these forms of mass were being shapeshifted without their own knowledge. Brainwashed, their shrunken minds were no match for their police state persona. They were the institution, taught to be racist, sexist, rapey, and do what they're told. '*Same story the crow told me,*' Belinda thought, though when she tuned back into the music, it was the fierce transition to *Slipknot*. Any moment, she felt they're knot could be untied.

One of the men had protocol to follow. He sat down with Belinda and Victor for more interrogation.

"We know where you got the mushrooms. Where'd you get the

marijuana?"

There was not a morsel of information to be had.

"Okay, fine. The judge will want to know, you can tell him. But how do you think you're going to go home today unless you tell us something."

All the goon could hear is silence. Victor and Belinda heard:

"Beautiful lie
You can pray
You can pay
Till you're buried alive
... Blackmailer blues
Everyone in the room
Owns a part of the noose."

"Look, you're both minors and even though this is your first offense, there is no way you are just going to walk out of here. It's time to call mommy and daddy, so who's going first?"

Victor wondered if he spit on him what would happen, but he saw the entire interplay in another dimension and knew he shouldn't. Belinda stared at his pores, the man wreaked of arm pit that smelled like dead meat and obsessive military training. She broke down his entire ego in her mind, this subhuman was a master of terror living in fear. Molded after the American patriot, he barely got his high school diploma and knew he didn't have to be smart to go into the Marines and subsequently, law enforcement. He saw the billboard about the hiring bonus, and it hit like he wished his numbers would in Vegas.

"Is this your address book?" he said to Belinda. She investigated him further and could see inside his crepe paper soul how he must hurt his children and beat his wife if she didn't have dinner on the table when he got home, and that he probably will never get to sodomize a man since that cross around his neck fit as tight as a hooker's choker.

She's not playing ball. He opens the tiny red soft plastic address book. "Oh, here's your name on the first page, must have something to do with you." He thumbs through it. "I bet someone in here will want to come pick you up." He goes through it page by page, "Benjamin, Brooke, Cindy, Christina, Carmein, Darren, Francesca," he loses patience, and flips further. "Who's it gonna be, Belinda?"

Not a word from her lips.

"Oh, look, Aunt Harriet, I bet she'll want to pick you up. Perfect, oh that area code is close." It was not close.

Belinda rolled her eyes and shook her head at Victor. He raised his shoulders, unsure about their next move.

The oaf went back to his desk and made the call. He mockingly recited his programmed script to her Aunt Harriet and put on all the friendly hero bullshit into it and hung up. "She's calling your mother for us, what a huge help."

About an hour and half later, Victor's dad arrived to pick them both up. There was a fanfare of phone calling behind the scenes, and ultimately it was up to Thomas to make the trek and bring them home. When he showed up an hour and a half later, the kids were starting to find space from the crux of their journey, and once their handcuffs were removed, they both knew how fortunate they were to have someone to take them out of there. They walked towards the door, and both looked back at Patrick. He gave them a happy smile and a nod, his eyes messaged, 'You did good.'

How One Young Man Did Not Spend the Rest of his Life in Prison

Levi was thirteen when he started taking LSD. It changed his life.

Across the street from his house lived a few hippies who would play guitar and hang out on the porch. Levi went over one day and a nice girl with flowers in her hair taught him how to make a rainbow-colored bracelet with embroidery string tied to his toes. He sat barefoot, with these hippie girls braiding bracelets while some guys were playing guitars and he thought, 'this is fucking awesome.' Everybody was happy.

Levi's role models in town were guys who wore leather jackets with knives sticking out of their boots. But he wanted to hang out with these people, these happy hippies. They gave him LSD and it changed the way he saw everything. The world was not how it seemed, and it was better in many ways. Hanging out with his new friends, he got to thinking about the world and how fucked up it seems to be. How terrible it was. It seemed taking LSD helped him make good choices in his life, so he decided that the world needed some help. He dedicated himself to selling LSD. Levi jumped into it in full effect. He discovered the music of the Grateful Dead amongst these hippies and went on Grateful Dead tour and raged LSD.

It took a few years but by the time he was seventeen, he was doing it tough. He was warned by many, "you're going to go to prison because you're fucking crazy."

He knew that was probably true, but he believed the fight that he was fighting was more than just himself and money. "This is a big deal," he told them, "I'm doing my thing. Thanks for the warning."

But they were right. He did go to prison.

A kid from Delaware was living in his VW bus in the panhandle. This kid was broke, running around asking everybody for acid and everybody was telling him to fuck off because he was such a bust. In 1990, the United States government's Drug Enforcement Administration started Operation Dead End and it was meant to take out all the psychedelics in the Grateful Dead scene. These subhumans wanted to put a stop to the whole thing with a bunch of federal money and agents. Levi was in the first wave to get caught up in this attack.

The kid went over to Berkeley, and by this time, the feds were getting ready to pull out because he had already incriminated the hell out of himself. They didn't need evidence to stick him on a conspiracy, but by chance, he ran into a friend of Levi's. The friend called Levi and two hours later he was at the hotel to meet him.

And the kid didn't have the money on him. Levi did not trust him enough to give him the product. "I have to go up there with you. It's a total violation of protocol," Levi explained. "You're supposed to have the money, but fuck, let's go."

Inside the hotel room, he stood around, trying to be patient with the kid sitting on the bed. The kid was anxious. Suddenly a guy barged in from an adjoining room. He was a fed, and it was a bust. Another fed came in and removed a small camera from the lamp. They were recording video the entire time the guys were in the room.

The fed grabbed Levi and arrested him with 22,000 hits of LSD. The kid had got busted on the east coast and told the feds he'd give up his supplier in California. The feds took them all down. That kid had never been in trouble before and he got put in a halfway house.

Levi got put into jail.

"They're talking about giving you forty years because you're a career criminal and they're going to charge you with conspiracy," Levi's lawyer told him. "My best advice to you is just plead guilty and take the twenty-three years that they're offering."

'Twenty-three years.' Levi thought about it. 'That is a fucking long time.' He asks her, "How come it's twenty-three years?"

"Oh, because they're weighing the paper. The feds say that your two grams of LSD is on paper that weighs 126 grams, therefore you will be sentenced for 126 grams of LSD."

That is like a quarter pound plus of raw crystal, distinctly different than two grams. It was a fucked-up deal, and they were doing it to everybody. Levi wasn't being singled out. Operation Dead End was in full effect and people were getting popped with ten vials of liquid and getting charged with 1000 grams because of the weight of the water.

Offered a plea bargain at twenty-three years, he took it. But somewhere deep inside his soul, Levi carried a tiny bit of hope that someday the sentencing guidelines would change. He told the judge, "I plead guilty to 22,000 hits but I am not pleading guilty to 126 grams. The prosecutor was indifferent since Levi was getting the same sentence. Turning twenty years old, he was shipped off to a maximum-security penitentiary to start his twenty-three-year bit.

Back at the halfway house, the kid meets a girl, and they fall in love. She is horrified by his situation and works with a newly formed organization called Families Against Mandatory Minimums (FAMM) and their grassroots campaign to publicize the disparity in the sentencing guidelines. The girl advocates for him and soon the media visits the kid. He's interviewed by the who's who of the evening news and becomes the face of the movement on cable one-hour specials, all to help reform LSD guidelines.

The lamp camera video of their bust is all over television. Everyone watched Levi get shoved by the feds and arrested. DEA insists they needed the buyer, or they'd never get to the supplier. They got both.

Levi owns up. He takes responsibility for his actions proudly. Inside, he conducts himself like a Shaolin warrior. He gets involved with the Native American church and does kundalini sweat lodges and yoga. He reads an amazing amount of literature. He gets the highest score ever in the department on his GED exam. He's hired to teach all the brothers to do math. He's serving his twenty-three years. When Levi reflects on his case in his cell, he remembered what the judge said. "If I had any way of not giving you this sentence, I would do so, but my hands are bound."

The publicity campaign against mandatory minimums moved forward. A scientist from a renown psychedelic research laboratory procured a sample of the LSD from the DEA scientists and conducts tests on Levi's acid. He concludes in his case, the LSD is not **absorbed** in the paper with the B but rather **adsorbed** on the paper with a D, and the subtle distinction of that is that adsorption is not considered to be mixed with, it is considered to be separate from, even if it's adhered to, analogous to a label on a beer bottle. It was enough for the judge to bite into, and he did. "Sounds good to me," the judge said in court.

Levi's sentence was reduced and recalculated. The Bureau of Prisons dropped his security level and he moved to a plush prison camp with no fences, doing nine years. The DEA scientist and the prosecutor were losing their minds. Like clockwork, they filed an appeal.

Every day, Levi woke up and thought, 'Is this the day I'm going to run away and not spend the rest of my life in prison? Or do I just sit here like an idiot and wait for the axe to fall?' It was harder than being in max prison by a long shot. He would've rather been surrounded by people doing three life sentences and killing each other, then surrounded by white collar criminals. He knew he had to stay put.

But the government won their appeal, and the Ninth Circuit told the judge to fuck off. Levi's original sentence was reinstated.

In Washington D.C., the pressure from the grassroots organizations of FAMM and other activists "inspired" two senators to write legislation to reform and specify that LSD was different than other drugs and paper should not be weighed nor the liquid. The legislation assigned a set uniform presumptive weight to each dosage unit of 400 micrograms regardless of the carrier medium, which is four times stronger than average but that's way better than the weight of the carrier medium. It was a bold stroke, no doubt with political motive, but showed slight mercy. The movement for reform had a victory at the capital in 1996.

Levi was sent to San Francisco. He arrived in a crowded court room with standing room only and an overflow in the hallway. This was a landmark case. The judge told Levi his new sentence was 70 months. "You've been in for 69, so you get immediate release," he proclaimed. The court room went crazy! Everybody was screaming and freaking out. The judge pounded his gavel to take back the room. "Order, order, I will clear this courtroom! Order, order!"

That's how one young man did not spend the rest of his life in prison.

One Hot Red Minute

Wendy walked down the avenue that afternoon with a couple guys Matthew had never seen before. As they came closer, he sized them up, tweakers with picked over faces, probably weighing in at a little over a buck ten.

"Wasssup?" she said, happy to see him. She always had a light on inside, even within all the darkness outside.

"Hey now, how you doin'? What's shakin'?"

"Nothing much. These are my friends, Joe, Ruben, and Casey."

"Hey man," Matthew said, being cordial.

"Hi," Joe mustered. The others seem socially awkward as fuck. Matthew figures Wendy must be making some good money off 'em, they look tore up, like they haven't slept for days.

"They're sleeping on my couch. They're playing the Penny Court tonight." The Penny Court was a frat house with custies, but not anywhere Matthew would normally hang out.

"Oh yeah?"

"Yeah, they're in a band called Red Minute. They just got signed, they're gonna be huge," she tells him

'Yeah, right motherfucker,' he thinks. All Matthew sees is three strung out tweaker dudes.

A lot of the kids on tour didn't have a place to go and some were abused, molested, and runaways. If they ended up on Dead tour, it wasn't a hundred percent that they were big fans, but by the time Matthew ended his first tour, he loved the Grateful Dead and was going to every show. Street kids had nowhere to go, but if they ended up on tour, they had better chances of making a living and having fun. And if they liked tour, they fell in love with a rocking band at the best party in the world.

Those kinds of kids ended up on Haight. A bunch of street kids with nowhere to go. Matthew clicked with those kids though his story was about selling drugs. But he hopped trains with the other gutter punks and traveled throughout the country, drinking, getting high, and doing whatever the fuck he wanted. Working corners selling bags, spare changing or busking with other kids if there was something to play, he made out okay. In between the adventures on the rail, he liked to hang out in Berkeley and stay on the streets. His friend Wendy sold speed and though he didn't do speed, she was good people. A cool friend for sure.

That afternoon Matthew hung out with a bunch of those freight train kids, including Kelly, Bart, and Kyle, a kid with long dreads who always wore a metal tee shirt. "So, what's up with that band? You know them?" Matthew said.

"Oh, they suck," Bart said, spitting a lug as far as he possibly could into the gutter. These were a crew of hardcore kids with high music standards.

"But there's going to be a bar," Kelly inserted.

"Shit let's go then," Matthew recommended.

Stomping through the city, drinking cheap cans of beer, they picked up a few more kids on the way, ate some acid, and formed a sturdy eight pack when they arrived at the frat house party. The large brown and orange three-story craftsman was old school Bezerkley for sure, with its huge front door and wraparound porch. Jarhead college kids crawled in every precipice of the structure drinking, smoking, and playing out their stupid higher education coming of age roles.

"He said that?"

"She was where?"

"I have never even talked to him before!"

"Well, I started pre-law, but philosophy is just a better path, more suitable to the way my mind really works. Oh, no, they hate it, my parents are pissed."

Conversation after conversation, the college kids were wavering between contrived seriousness and overt performance. And they were all in formal wear. Fancy suits, tuxedos, and big dresses swished all over the premises.

Pirate, this punk rocker kid who went by Pirate because he had the black pointy boots, pegged pants, leather jacket, and spiky hair, walked inside with zero reservations looking for the bar. In a large dining room in the middle of the ground floor, a massive wood bar was shoved near the wall. The classic makeshift house party bar. No one tended, but it was stacked, a DIY operation with plenty of choices. Pirate jumps over this bar, swipes two bottles of whiskey and hands them over to Matthew and Kelly.

"Hey, you can't do that." a pimply, cheesy tuxedo'd frat boy sternly objects.

Pirate looks into his J.Crew soul. "What are you talking about? I just did." He hops back over, and the crew gets comfortable on a large tan puffed leather couch. Passing the bottles around, no one else says a thing to them.

The dresses turned into bells of color, swiping past one another, often pressing close to the black satin legs of trousers, and the fancy interplay was increasingly psychedelic. Matthew drank and drank. The crew was getting hammered. He watched the college kids trail off in one direction and another, colors splashing through the space like a brush on a canvas. Leaning back on the couch next to him, Bart drifted off, the high so encompassing he needed to close his eyes for a spell. He finally sat up, and as immediate as a fire hydrant hit by a speeding car in a seventies movie, he projectile vomited across the room.

About eight feet away, a woman in a silk mesh and rayon dress is hit! She screams, “So gross!” Bart finished and leaned back into the couch and passed right back out. The woman shrieked and stormed out of the house. Kelly and Matthew crack up laughing. Pirate and the rest of the crew can’t stop laughing. They’re tripping hard!

So hard, they never saw Red Minute play, but Matthew thought he could hear the band through the walls playing in the room next door.

HOMEMADE

The Panhandle was getting way too sketchy. Between the cops and the gangsters showing up posing to buy bags and ripping the kids off, these were dark days. But the kids hung on, dodging bullets, some taking 'em.

Cody skated all over the Haight, he was never looking for custies, instead he just hung out and made himself available. Sometimes he made some connections on his pager and waited for people to show up. He had more than his share of close calls with thieves, often having to judge them as they made eye contact and approached—he'd shake his head no real quick and walk the other way towards some tourists or into a store.

Joanie stayed up in their VW bus, parked a ways up behind Buena Vista. She made embroidery patches and crocheted tams waiting for him, the time was crucial for her to work uninterrupted. One morning after he skated down to the panhandle she got an idea.

Surprised to see her coming down the street, Cody smiled wide. She was magic, and always made him happy.

"Hey there," she said.

"Well, hello, to what do I owe this enchanted visit?" he responded.

"I made you something. Let me see your skateboard." He handed it over to her and she turned her back away from the street and applied two strips of Velcro underneath the board. She revealed a small handmade pouch from her pocket and showed Cody her invention.

"Just keep this on the bottom of your skateboard when its

sketchy around. That way if the cops come and search you or anyone tries to gaffle, the pouch will be facing the ground, and they won't see it." She stuck it to the Velcro and then ripped it off and on, it was perfect.

"I love you," he said.

"I know," she replied and kissed him on the lips.

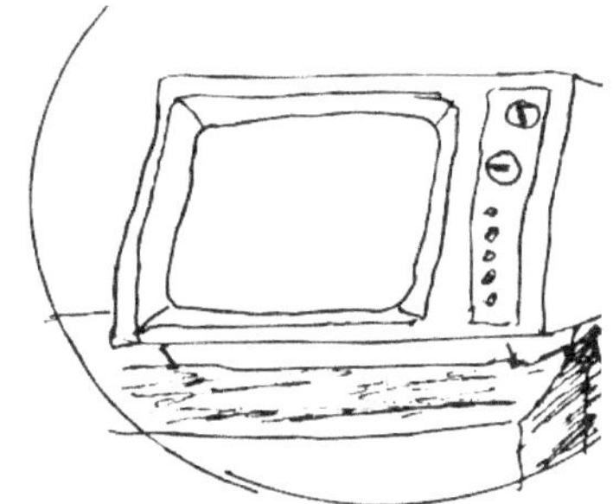

Streets of San Francisco

After a day swingin' bags in San Francisco, sometimes the kids would take the BART and stay by the Coliseum at the Days Inn. If you have a good day and make some cash, you're staying somewhere else. In the city, a hotel room costs anywhere from twenty to sixty bucks. Sixty could get a nice, fat room. If you could get five bucks a person, that's a real nice room.

There was a small cheap two-story hotel off Lombard with rooms for about forty dollars a night. The entrance is on the seaside, with an office on the left, and a courtyard with parking down below. It's a sleepy spot. Not a lot of drama, just TV's and beds.

This night, Tristan and Colleen stayed on Lombard and got a room.

In the morning, they drank the so-so hotel room coffee watching old TV show reruns and *Streets of San Francisco* comes on. Smoking a fattie, they're absorbed in the plot: a man chases some dude down a windy section of Lombard, right down the street from where they are.

Tristan sits up and says, "It's right down there." On the show, a man pulls a car up fast and gets out and runs up to a hotel. It's this hotel. "They look like their running right over here!" he screams. They watch the hero run right into the hotel and up the stairs and they brace themselves, tightening up as the dude on TV runs into the very same room they are in!

Tristan remembers the room number, the same room number he saw as he walked into the door earlier. Lying on the bed, in the same room, in the same hotel watching TV.

"What are the odds on that?" Colleen wonders.

ABOUT THE AUTHOR

Trina Calderón is an author, journalist, and TV-filmmaker. She's worked with visual artists making documentaries, and writing articles, essays, books, and museum and gallery exhibits. Specializing in counterculture storytelling, she wrote the ground-breaking exhibit, *Pump Me Up: DC Subcultures of the 1980's*, at the Corcoran Gallery of Art in Washington, D.C., the first comprehensive look at the real frenzy of culture inside the capital. Cementing the legacy of graffiti art, she helped write and produce *WALL WRITERS: Graffiti in its Innocence*, a massive book and documentary feature film about the American art innovators. For the 35th anniversary of D.C.'s infamous 9:30 Club, she helped write and compile the large oral history book, *9:30: A Time and a Place*. She's been published in *Juxtapoz Magazine, Rolling Stone, The Believer* and more. Born and raised in Los Angeles, California, she lives amongst the frogs and the oak trees where the mountain meets the sea.